GET ALL T

WITH JUST ONE PROOF OF PURCHASE:

$50 VALUE

◆ **Hotel Discounts** up to 60% at home and abroad ◆ **Travel Service -** Guaranteed lowest published airfares plus 5% cash back on tickets ◆ **$25 Travel Voucher** ◆ **Sensuous Petite Parfumerie** collection ◆ **Insider Tips Letter** with sneak previews of upcoming books

You'll get a FREE personal card, too. It's your passport to all these benefits– and to even more great gifts & benefits to come!

There's no club to join. No purchase commitment. No obligation.

SS-PP5A

Enrollment Form

☐ *Yes!* I WANT TO BE A *Privileged Woman*.
Enclosed is one *PAGES & PRIVILEGES*™ Proof of
Purchase from any Harlequin or Silhouette book currently for
sale in stores (Proofs of Purchase are found on the back pages
of books) and the store cash register receipt. Please enroll me
in *PAGES & PRIVILEGES*™. Send my Welcome Kit and FREE
Gifts -- and activate my FREE benefits -- immediately.
More great gifts and benefits to come.

NAME (please print)

ADDRESS   APT. NO

CITY   STATE   ZIP/POSTAL CODE

Please allow 6-8 weeks for delivery. Quantities are limited. We reserve the right to
substitute items. Enroll before October 31, 1995 and receive one full year of benefits.

Name of store where this book was purchased_____

Date of purchase_____

Type of store:
☐ Bookstore   ☐ Supermarket   ☐ Drugstore
☐ Dept. or discount store (e.g. K-Mart or Walmart)
☐ Other (specify)_____

Which Harlequin or Silhouette series do you usually read?

_____

Complete and mail with one Proof of Purchase and store receipt to:
U.S.: *PAGES & PRIVILEGES*™, P.O. Box 1960, Danbury, CT 06813-1960
Canada: *PAGES & PRIVILEGES*™, 49-6A The Donway West, P.O. 813,
North York, ON M3C 2E8

SS-PP5B

▼ DETACH HERE AND MAIL TODAY! ▼

HOW TO KNOW YOU'RE LUCKY THE GROOM GOT AWAY:

1. Your beautiful white bouquet wilts as soon as it's handed to you.

2. Those aren't tears of joy welling up in your eyes.

3. The heirloom necklace around your neck suddenly slips off as you walk down the aisle.

4. A handsome stranger bursts into the church and sends your fiancé fleeing.

Dear Reader,

We have a very special treat in store for you this month. Many of you have been following the Always a Bridesmaid! continuity series from line to line within Silhouette. Now it's Shadows' turn, and veteran author Jane Toombs rises to the challenge in *The Abandoned Bride*.

You would think that being left at the altar would be about the most awful thing that could happen to a woman. But just the opposite turns out to be true for Lucy Maguire. Because Max Ryder's surprise entrance into the church sends her groom-to-be fleeing—and lands Max right where he belongs: in the middle of Lucy's life.

Next month follow Always a Bridesmaid! to its exciting conclusion in Silhouette Special Edition, where Sherryl Woods pens *Finally A Bride,* a book you *won't* want to miss. And come back to Shadows next month, too, for more of the irresistible dark side of love.

Until then—enjoy!

Leslie Wainger
Senior Editor and Editorial Coordinator

Please address questions and book requests to:
Silhouette Reader Service
U.S.: 3010 Walden Ave., P.O. Box 1325, Buffalo, NY 14269
Canadian: P.O. Box 609, Fort Erie, Ont. L2A 5X3

Jane Toombs
The Abandoned Bride

SILHOUETTE® Shadows™

Published by Silhouette Books
America's Publisher of Contemporary Romance

SILHOUETTE BOOKS

ISBN 0-373-27056-9

THE ABANDONED BRIDE

CAST OF CHARACTERS

The Women:

Hannah Farley: Blue-blooded bad girl.

Emma Wynn: Once burned, twice shy.

Sophie Reynolds: Single mom with secrets.

Lucy Maguire: Not left at the altar for long.

Katie Jones: Always a bridesmaid…

The Men:

Matthew Granger: Stranger in a small town.

Michael Flint: Mr. Wrong has never been so right.

Ford Maguire: Lucy's lawman brother falls for shady lady?

Max Ryder: Mystery man appears in the nick of time.

Luke Cassidy: Single dad makes impassioned plea.

Why does Lucy's groom-to-be abandon her at the altar the minute Max bursts into the church? Who *is* Max, anyway? And those aren't tears of joy running down Katie's cheeks when Luke proposes marriage—why isn't she happy that she'll finally be a bride?

Books by Jane Toombs

Silhouette Shadows

Return to Bloodstone House #5
Dark Enchantment #12
What Waits Below #16
The Volan Curse #35
The Woman in White #50
*The Abandoned Bride #56

* Always a Bridesmaid!

JANE TOOMBS

believes that a touch of the mysterious adds spice to a romance. Her childhood fascination with stories about shape-changers such as vampires, werewolves and shamans never faded, leading to her present interest in supernatural influences, not only in Gothic romances but in the early cultures of all peoples.

A Californian transplanted to New York, Jane lives in the shadow of Storm King Mountain.

CHAPTER ONE

Standing in the small anteroom of St. John's Church, with rain pattering against the high and tiny window, Lucy Maguire struggled to fasten her grandmother's moonstone necklace around her neck, disarranging strands of her long, dark hair, setting her veil askew and making herself more jittery than she already was—if that was possible.

The necklace was old, but she'd recently had its intricate clasp repaired, so it shouldn't be giving her this much trouble. Could the difficulty she was having be a sign she was making a mistake? Squeezing her eyes shut, as if by doing so she could also close her mind to negative thoughts, Lucy told herself firmly that all brides had last-minute misgivings.

More than likely she was fumbling with the clasp because she felt guilty about her impulsive decision to substitute the moonstones for the sapphire-and-diamond necklace that was Joe's bridal gift to her. She would explain later to him how she needed the moonstones for the traditional "something old"—even if that wasn't the entire reason she was wearing them. Her grandmother, she felt, would have wanted her to.

"Here, let me help."

Katie Jones's voice and the touch of her hands brought Lucy back from her guilt trip. "Thanks," she said, relinquishing the fastening to Katie, who like her other bridesmaids, was wearing a blue gown.

Joe had chosen the color; he preferred blue to any other. "Blue brings out the madonna in you," he'd told her, "and I definitely don't mean the singer."

His words reminded her that the sapphires in the necklace he'd given her were supposed to be her "something blue." Should she change necklaces? It wasn't too late. However, she didn't really need the sapphires, because she was wearing a blue garter....

"There," Katie said. When Lucy turned to thank her, Katie readjusted the bridal veil and then nodded in satisfaction. "Perfect. You're all set."

Was she, though? The organ music swelled, her cue to appear. As Lucy hesitated, she heard one of her bridesmaids murmur that rain wasn't lucky on a wedding day.

"Lucy already has all the luck she needs," another insisted. "She's marrying Joe Dooley, isn't she?"

Yes, she *was* lucky. Out of all the single women in Clover, Joe had chosen her. So why didn't she stop dithering and dwell, instead, on how fortunate she was? Taking a deep breath and easing it out, Lucy left the anteroom.

At the back of the church, her brother, waiting to lead her to the altar, winked at her, a left-eyed wink, one of their secret signals from Lucy's childhood, meaning "don't worry, you're okay and you'll do just fine." Though she might have preferred the right-eyed "everything is totally okay" wink, Lucy knew better than to expect it, because Ford had made it clear that he thought she'd rushed pell-mell into this marriage with Joe.

Lucy's chin came up. Ford had been both father and mother to her after their parents were killed when she was nine. At twenty-seven she was hardly a child and certainly more than capable of making her own decisions. She'd agreed to marry Joe today and marry him she would, rain or shine. Holding her bouquet of white roses in her right hand, she rested her left on her brother's arm and together they walked slowly down the aisle.

Despite her affirmation of what she was doing, Lucy felt distinctly odd—not exactly in a daze but as though she were both in St. John's Church and, at the same time, somewhere else. The organ music seemed faint and far-off as did the rustles and murmurs of the guests in the pews. For some reason she could no longer smell the thin fragrance of the hothouse roses she carried or the floral perfume she wore, even though she'd dabbed on more than usual. Through a haze she saw Joe standing at the altar, waiting for his bride. For her? It didn't seem possible.

Struggling to pull herself together, Lucy refused to let herself believe the strangeness might be the prelude to something she dreaded, something she had hoped and prayed would never come to her again. Nothing could be more unwelcome than a return of the childhood visions she'd once been subject to. Why, she asked herself, after so many years of lying quiescent, would such a thing return to plague her?

This was no time to succumb to anything so troublesome, so she thrust her apprehension from her mind and fixed her gaze on Joe, determined to think of nothing else but him, Joseph Dooley, soon to be her husband. How could he possibly look so relaxed and confident? Apparently he had no doubts at all, but then he rarely did. No doubts about what was right for him and no doubts about what was best for her. In the same way he'd insisted blue was her color, he'd told her she must always wear her hair long and straight and parted in the middle.

"I love that pure and innocent look of yours," he'd said, while doing his best to seduce her.

His attempt had amused Lucy. Not that she'd objected to the seduction. Or at least she hadn't realized it until she'd found that even though she enjoyed Joe's kisses, she wasn't ready to make love with him. Not then and not later, either.

She was assuring herself she'd feel differently after they were married, when, to her horror, the white rosebuds in her bouquet began to wither before her eyes, turning brown, then black with decay. Which was impossible. As she'd feared, she was having a vision.

While she struggled to rid herself of the vision and to banish the unpleasant sight of the roses, Lucy felt the clasp of the moonstone necklace give way. Before she could make any preventative move, the necklace slipped down, falling onto her bouquet, where it nestled among the roses, roses now as fresh and white as ever. Relief that the vision appeared to be over and that she hadn't caused a scene overcame her distress. Had anyone noticed? Her brother? Joe?

A glance at Ford assured her that although his expression might be a tad grim, it reflected his feeling about the wedding in general and not about anything unusual in her behavior. As she focused on Joe, he looked away from her, his attention shifting to the back of the church, where, from the noise, some late-comer seemed to be forcefully opening the closed entrance doors.

Keeping her gaze on Joe, she watched uncomprehendingly as his expression changed from complacency to consternation. For a long minute he didn't move, staring at whoever had entered, then, to her complete amazement, he dashed toward the side entrance of the church, flung open the door and vanished through it.

Footsteps pounded down the aisle. Lucy turned and saw a tall, rugged man in black, a stranger, rush past her with near hurricane force and fling himself through the side door, obviously in pursuit of Joe. Ford cursed, shook himself loose from her and ran after the two men.

Stranded alone near the altar, Lucy stared at the open side door in shocked bewilderment. What was happening? Who was the man in black? Why had Joe fled from him?

Like a wreath of bluebells, her bridesmaids encircled her. Katie's arm came around her waist and she gently urged Lucy back down the aisle, where, to either side, voices rose and fell as the wedding guests discussed the amazing event.

"Burst in here like the devil himself," a woman said.

"Only guilty men run," a man insisted.

"What I'd like to know is which one the sheriff was after," another said.

The sheriff. Her brother, Ford. He'd sort things out and then everything would be all right. Wouldn't it?

Lucy didn't realize her hands were shaking until the bridal bouquet slipped from her quivering fingers and fell onto the carpeted aisle, dislodging the moonstone necklace. The two of them paused while Katie picked up the roses and the necklace and offered them to Lucy. She refused the roses, but took the moonstones, clutching the necklace.

As they moved on, she noticed Luke Cassidy sitting in a pew to her left with his wide-eyed son in his lap. Next to her, Katie drew in her breath and her step faltered. Though caught up in her own distress, Lucy momentarily wondered if Katie was upset about seeing Luke with the boy. But why would she be? An instant later Lucy froze, staring in disbelief as Luke Cassidy's features shifted and changed until another man entirely sat in the pew holding the same child. She blinked and shuddered.

"We're almost there—please don't faint," Katie murmured in her ear.

With Katie's words, Lucy's vision vanished, leaving Luke again holding his son. No more, she pleaded mutely as she and Katie pushed through the throng of guests now leaving the church. She couldn't take any more.

Once they were secluded in the anteroom, the wedding party commiserated with Lucy, until she thought she would scream. While she appreciated their concern, she knew they didn't really understand why she was so disturbed. How could they, when nobody in the world knew of her visions? Naturally she was upset over what had occurred—no bride relishes being deserted at the altar, no matter what the circumstances. But her confidence in her brother mitigated her distress over Joe's defection. Somehow or other, she felt, Ford would straighten out the confusion.

Lucy was grateful when Katie commandeered one of the ushers to drive her home to her cottage. Once alone behind her own closed door, Lucy removed her veil and then her gown, carefully hanging it in the closet before collapsing onto the bed in her slip. No tears came. Instead she brooded over the visions.

Why had they returned? She really was more distraught by their reappearance in her life than she was by Joe's flight. Though no one suspected she had them, if the visions continued, how long would it be before those over thirty began to whisper about her being ''a tad tetched in the head'' the way old Letitia Franklin had been during the last few years of her life?

Those her age and younger would be even blunter.

She hadn't suffered through a vision since she was nine years old and that vision had been so terrible she'd prayed it would never happen again. Ford dismissed that vision as a nightmare. She'd wanted to believe him but never quite could.

She hadn't known how to begin to explain the strangeness of what had happened to her so she didn't even try after that. But she never again spoke to anyone about what she'd seen on that awful night. How happy she'd been when no more visions plagued her. But now they'd returned. On her wedding day.

No, that wasn't quite right. In truth, what she'd had three months ago might well have been the beginning, though at the time she'd closed her mind against the possibility her dreaded visions might be surfacing again. Even now she couldn't be sure whether what she'd experienced then actually was a vision.

It had happened back in November on the day she'd met Joe Dooley for the very first time....

After two days of rain, Lucy appreciated the warmth of the November sun as she strolled along Santee Street on her way toward the center of town. She paused to savor the sweet scent of the late roses still blooming behind the Pennyworths' wrought-iron fence and noted Roger, the sleek black-and-white cat, dozing on the porch steps.

"I'd better not hear you yowling under my window again at three in the morning," she warned.

Roger slitted his eyes, gave her a look that told her very plainly she didn't scare him one bit and then resumed his nap.

Lucy walked on toward the main street, heading for Katz's Jewelry Store, where she planned to leave her grandmother's moonstone necklace so Mr. Katz could repair the old, broken clasp. She'd all but forgotten about the necklace until she'd dreamed about her grandmother two nights ago.

In the dream, her grandmother looked just the same as she had in the only photograph Lucy had ever seen of her, dressed in red with her gray-streaked dark hair fluffed like a halo around her head. As a child Lucy had overheard her mother telling her father that in her opinion it was just as well Grandma Maguire had died young. Eccentric was one thing but weird was another.

"You told me she was estranged from your family," Lucy's mother had added, "so I wasn't prepared when she appeared unexpectedly at our wedding, looking like some ancient Greek oracle in that peculiar red velvet gown. Or do I mean Irish banshee? I couldn't decide whether I was more embarrassed or frightened. I do know I nearly fainted when she announced to everyone within earshot that she was leaving her moonstone necklace to our daughter. Why we didn't yet know if we'd ever even have any children!"

But in Lucy's dream, Grandma Maguire hadn't seemed at all threatening.

"You are no longer a child," Grandma said to her in the dream.

"I'm not a child," she acknowledged.

"So now it is time," Grandma told her. "Time for you to wear the necklace I bequeathed to you and you alone on your ninth birthday because you were born on July 21, born on the cusp, as I was. What have you done with the moonstones, Lucy?"

"The necklace is safe in my jewelry box. The clasp broke the first and last time I tried to wear it, when I was nine." That had been the night her parents died. Because of what had happened, Lucy hadn't so much as looked at the moonstones since then.

"The clasp always breaks when the necklace is passed on, to give the stones a chance to adjust to their new owner, to allow them to absorb her essence so they can protect her. The moonstones have come to know you well. Repair the clasp, Lucy. The time has come for you to wear the necklace."

The dream had been so vivid that when Lucy roused she thought for a moment or two she could smell the rose scent Mother had once said Grandma Maguire used. Time to wear the necklace again? How could she?

Later that day Lucy decided it was her guilty conscience speaking to her in the dream. If her grandmother hadn't deeded her the small cottage where she now lived, she would not have been able to be on her own. Not to mention bequeathing her what must be a valuable necklace. The least she could do was get the clasp fixed so she could wear it.

Mr. Katz would soon solve that problem, allowing Grandmother to rest in peace along with her own guilty conscience. Actually the necklace—seven lustrous moonstones set at intervals along a thick gold chain with filigreed gold beads between them—was quite striking, though a tad heavy.

The moonstone, if she remembered correctly, was the stone of love—but only if the wearer was born between June 22 and July 21. Lucy sighed. Twenty-seven years old and she'd never been in love, not really. Once or twice she'd thought maybe she was, but her brother had managed to break up each romance before she'd had the chance to find out one way or the other. *Overprotective* was the word for Ford.

A display in the window of Masterson's Memorabilia caught her eye and she paused to look at the old movie posters propped side by side without regard for who was next to whom—Shirley Temple's dimpled smile beamed sunnily cheek by jowl with Bela Lugosi's sinister and hypnotic Dracula stare. Amused, Lucy started to turn away, but halted abruptly to avoid running into the man who had ever so silently come up beside her.

Inexplicably, a wave of dizziness gripped her. When she recovered enough to be coherent, she started to apologize, but when she looked at him, her polite

"Excuse me" died on her tongue. Hair rose on her nape as she stared at not Bela Lugosi, many years dead, but at the undead Dracula himself. He reached for her; she gasped in terror and shrank back, losing her balance. His hand closed over her arm.

The moment he touched her, the Dracula image vanished as though it had never been, and she found herself gazing into Joe Dooley's handsome face. They'd never been formally introduced, but she knew who he was—every woman in town did.

Scarlet with embarrassment—he must consider her crazy—Lucy tried to think of something to say, but she was speechless.

"I'm sorry," he said. "I didn't mean to startle you."

"I—I didn't know you were there," she managed to stammer. He really was the best-looking man she'd ever seen.

"I do apologize."

He smiled at her, a dazzling display of white teeth against his tan.

"Please let me make amends by inviting you to have coffee with me." He nodded toward Peg's Diner, just down the street.

"Why, thanks," she said, still flustered by what had happened and wondering uneasily if it had anything to do with those childhood visions she thought she'd left behind forever. "But it really isn't necessary."

"That's where you're wrong. I've been trying to meet you ever since I arrived in Clover, trying without success. Now that I finally have you in my clutches, Ms. Lucy Maguire, I won't let you escape easily."

She gazed at him, surprised that he knew her name. He'd wanted to meet *her?* Joe Dooley, the new and most fascinating man in town, the guy all her women friends were drooling over?

"If you insist," she said, realizing belatedly that she sounded as prim as any caricature of the old-maid librarian. Since she did work in the library and she wasn't married, she flushed. Talk about getting off on the wrong foot!

"Would you prefer a formal introduction first?" he asked, his smile robbing the words of any sting.

"I know who you are," she told him. "Coffee at Peg's is fine."

As they walked together to the diner, Lucy was aware of the side glances they attracted and knew it would be all over town before tonight that she'd been seen with Joe Dooley. She smiled, pleased with what could only be regarded as a coup on her part.

"You have a wonderful smile," he told her. "It hints of secrets waiting to be discovered."

"I'm afraid you're wrong. No one can keep a secret for very long here in Clover, and I'm certainly no exception."

He shook his head. "Everyone has a secret that they'd sooner take to the grave than reveal. As I'm sure my late great-aunt Letitia must have done. We never met, you know."

"I've heard that." Rumor also had it that Letitia Franklin had left him, as Ford said, a bundle.

"Have you ever been to the house?" Joe asked as he opened the door of the diner.

She knew he meant the Franklin mansion and she shook her head. "Ms. Franklin tended to be a recluse."

Their entrance, Lucy saw, was noted by everyone present. Once they were settled into a booth, Peg herself breezed over to take their order.

"Nice to see you, Lucy," she said. "And you, Mr. Dooley."

"'Joe,'" he said. "Just plain 'Joe.' I feel at home here, Peg."

Peg seemed as mesmerized by his smile as Lucy had been earlier. "That's right kind of you," she told him. "We're glad to have you here in town."

As they drank their coffee and talked, Lucy began to relax and enjoy his company. Apparently he hadn't labeled her a weirdo, as she'd feared he might after the way she'd behaved outside Masterson's. In fact, he didn't act as though he'd noticed anything out of the ordinary.

She couldn't deny she was flattered by his attention. Who wouldn't be? Tall, dark and handsome, Joe was by all odds the most eligible bachelor in town. And charming, as well.

"I suppose by morning they'll have us engaged," he said after Peg had refilled his cup for the third time.

Lucy, taken aback, almost choked on her coffee. He was absolutely right, but she hadn't expected him to actually say such a thing.

"I'm beginning to wish it were true," he added.

She couldn't believe he was serious, so she laughed.

He leaned across the table, catching her gaze and holding it, his dark eyes unfathomable. "I warned you

I wouldn't let you escape," he said softly. "I meant exactly that."

Lucy, enthralled, decided he really *was* as interested in her as she was him. She'd never met a man remotely like Joe Dooley. Ford might try, she told herself, but even he wouldn't be able to find anything wrong with Joe.

She was wrong.

"You hardly know the guy," her brother stopped by the library to tell her the next day. "Go easy until you get better acquainted. He may be okay, but there's something about his eyes I don't like."

"He's got beautiful eyes," Lucy insisted.

"All I noticed was they're sort of shifty," Ford said.

"Shifty!" Lucy's voice rose and she hurriedly dropped it to a lower level. "You're just trying to find fault with him."

Ford sighed. "Maybe so. Maybe I don't think any guy I've met so far is good enough for my baby sister. But do me a favor and take it slow with Joe—okay?"

"Until you finish checking him out, you mean."

He ruffled her hair. "You know me too well."

Lucy watched him leave, thinking that despite how much she loved her brother, he could make her angrier than anyone she knew. Maybe it was because he was the sheriff that he seemed to suspect every male who came on to her was, if not a proven criminal, a potential one, but his attitude infuriated her. She intended to go right on seeing Joe as much and as often as he wanted.

That is, if Ford didn't succeed in scaring him off. He'd certainly done that before to more than one potential suitor.

*   *   *

Lucy sprang up from the bed. Enough mooning over the past. She'd never been a person who collapsed in a crisis, and she damn well wouldn't begin now. Ford hadn't scared Joe off, but someone else certainly had, and she meant to find out who and why.

Moping about in her underwear definitely wasn't the way to begin. She dropped the necklace, shed all her wedding finery and pulled on jeans and a T-shirt. Noticing the moonstone necklace, coiled on the nightstand next to her bridal bouquet, she picked it up and worked the clasp, finding nothing wrong. Maybe Katie hadn't hooked it together quite right.

Eyeing the bouquet with distaste, she decided she really didn't wish to look at it ever again. Hurrying out her back door, she shredded the roses into her compost heap, barely aware that the rain had stopped. Her next-door neighbor's cat sauntered over to see if Lucy was discarding anything edible and she glowered at the female tabby. "If Polly would get your tubes tied or whatever it is they do to cats, you wouldn't attract every tom in the neighborhood, and I'd get some sleep."

The tabby rubbed against her ankles, purring.

"Never mind making up to me," Lucy muttered. "I'm contemplating saving up enough money so I can kidnap you and personally take you to the vet to be spayed."

Crumpling the unrecyclable parts of the bouquet, Lucy sat on the damp grass near the compost heap and began to pet the cat. "You shouldn't have anything to do with those toms," she told the tabby. "Males can't be trusted."

She should have listened to her brother. Ford's vague suspicions of Joe certainly seemed to have some foundation. Why otherwise would Joe have fled at the sight of that man in black? Lucy shook her head. Where was her sense of loyalty? Maybe she was too quick to condemn Joe. There might be a logical explanation for his disappearance.

Ford had gone after the two men, and if she knew her brother, he wouldn't be satisfied until he found out exactly what was going on. It could be the man in black was the one in the wrong, couldn't it? Before she condemned Joe, she would wait and hear what Ford had to say.

And there was always the chance that Joe would contact her and explain. She must keep an open mind. He'd told her over and over again how much he loved her and how he wanted nothing else in this world except to make her his wife. She'd believed him.

And she loved him in return. Didn't she? Frowning, Lucy looked down at the cat. "Do I love Joe Dooley or not?" she asked the tabby.

"I hope to hell and back that your answer is no."

Ford's voice jolted Lucy and she glanced up to see her brother standing framed in her open back door. Putting the cat aside, she rose and hurried to the house.

Moments later, brother and sister faced each other in her kitchen. "Where's Joe?" she demanded.

He shrugged. "Who knows? Not me and not Max Ryder."

"Is Max Ryder the man in black?"

"The what? You mean the guy in the church? Yeah, Ryder's his name. He's a PI."

Lucy, familiar with police jargon, knew that meant private investigator. "Why did he chase Joe from the church?"

"You know that wasn't the way it happened. Joe saw him and took off. Naturally Ryder went after him. He's been trying to nail Joe for months. And for good reason."

Lucy put her hands on her hips. "What reason?"

"I can't tell you. It's confidential. You'll have to trust me until I look into the situation and get down to the nitty-gritty."

Ignoring her belligerent stance, he reached out and put an arm around her, drawing her close. "Look, Sis, I know you're upset and I don't blame you. You have every right to be. But don't take it out on me. As soon as I can, I'll tell you everything. Right now, believe me when I say you were damn lucky that Ryder showed up before you said 'I do.'"

CHAPTER TWO

Lucy spent a weekend of soul-searching and fending off phone calls—even one from her best friend, Katie. She wasn't yet ready to talk about what had happened in the church. On Monday she called the library where she worked.

"I remember Ada saying she wanted some time off," Lucy told the head librarian, Marian Furlong. "I'd just as soon not take the next two weeks off as scheduled, so if Ada wants to go on vacation, I'd be glad to take her place."

"Are you sure you feel up to it?" Marian, who'd been one of the wedding guests, sounded taken aback.

"I'm positive," Lucy said firmly, hoping the call wouldn't turn into a discussion of what had happened or questions about whether she'd heard from Joe.

She hadn't yet. Though she still hoped Joe would eventually contact her with his explanation of why he'd run out on their wedding, she wasn't counting on it. And she certainly didn't intend to mope around during the two weeks of what was supposed to have been their honeymoon, waiting for a phone call or a visit from him. At the moment, what she needed was to return to work.

Marian agreed to call her back after talking to Ada, and when she did, she told Lucy to come to work the next day. "Ada wanted me to thank you for offering the time to her," Marian added, "though she was sorry, as we all are, about—well, everything."

They hung up. No one could be sorrier than Lucy was. And yet, somehow, once she'd gotten over the initial shock she really didn't feel devastated. She was reluctant to admit, even to herself, that relief was intermingled with her upset. Maybe she hadn't been quite as eager to marry Joe as she'd believed.

What would she do if he called this very second, offered a reasonable explanation for deserting her, then asked her to set another date for their wedding? Without having to ponder the question, she found the answer waiting: she would put him off. She would wait, exactly as Ford had urged her to do in the first place.

Lucy grimaced. How infuriating to have her brother proven right. Again.

The next morning she walked briskly to the library, sheltering from the rain under her umbrella. But once she arrived, she found no shelter from the speculative looks or the questions from co-workers and library patrons alike. She repeated "I don't know" so many times during the day that she almost said it to Marian when the librarian offered her a ride home after work.

Looks and questions tapered off during the days that followed, and people began treating her almost normally again. Much as she appreciated that, when she was alone at home she couldn't help but dwell on her failed wedding. Ford had promised to let her know more about why the man in black was after Joe as soon as he'd talked to Max Ryder again. But when she'd called her brother, all he had to say was that

Ryder hadn't yet returned to Clover because he was still searching for Joe. Ford had also checked Ryder out and found he was exactly what he said he was—a licensed PI.

Two weeks passed. The tabby next door, no longer in heat, stopped being a magnet for the local tomcats, making for quieter nights if not especially peaceful ones. On the weekend Lucy donned her oldest jeans, rejected a blue T-shirt for a yellow one and mowed her lawn, then sprawled on the webbed lounge in her backyard. She'd no more than gotten comfortable, when the tabby jumped onto her stomach and gazed solemnly at her.

"Don't look so smug," Lucy warned, scratching the cat behind the ears. "Another couple of months and you'll be feeding kittens again. Don't you dare plan to have them in my shed the way you did last time. You ought to know that's not the best place to bring up a family."

The far-from-new shed near her back property line had once been the shelter for a horse, Lucy knew, and she thought it rather picturesque, though Ford kept threatening to demolish it, claiming the shed was an eyesore. He did agree the five-room saltbox cottage their grandmother had left her was a jewel and had helped her paint it last summer. She gazed at the white siding gleaming in the sun, admiring the contrast of the green shutters.

The truth was she far preferred her simple cottage to the Franklin mansion on Highgate Road, spacious and luxurious as it was. Joe had insisted they live there, and if the wedding had come off as planned, she would be moving into the mansion now, the honeymoon over. Actually Joe had given her a key, and her suitcase and carry-on bag were still at the mansion, left there before the wedding. Though she didn't immediately need anything from the luggage, the stuff *was* hers.

"I'll have to drive out and bring my things home," she told the cat, wondering why the idea didn't appeal to her. Was it because the act was like writing *finis* to any thought of ever becoming Joe's wife?

The cat's eyes opened and she swiveled her head to look toward the brick path leading around the house from the front. Lucy followed the tabby's gaze and sat up abruptly. The man in black—black jeans and T-shirt this time—stood not more than ten feet away, staring at her with cold, pale-blue eyes, making her feel oddly vulnerable. What was he doing in her yard?

She eased the cat away from her and rose, intending to demand a reason for his presence. Before she could begin, she saw the reason—Ford—stride along the path and pause beside Max. Max, she noticed, topped Ford by maybe an inch. He was as ruggedly built as she recalled and his expression every bit as grim as when he'd invaded the church. Though no one would call him handsome, he had a face that, to use her friend Katie's Aunt Peg's words, was "full of character."

As a child, Lucy had asked Peg what she meant by that.

"I mean the person's face shows he or she has learned life's hard lessons and come out the better for it," Peg had told her—which hadn't helped Lucy much at the time.

But gazing at Max—she couldn't seem to look away—she understood exactly what Katie's aunt had been trying to convey. Which didn't mean Lucy liked him. Or trusted him.

"He hasn't been here," Max said.

She knew he was speaking to her brother, even though he remained intent on her. Nor had he asked a question.

She answered anyway. "If you mean Joe, I haven't seen or heard from him. Thanks to you." Her voice carried the bitterness she felt.

"Don't mind my kid sister," Ford said, moving toward Lucy while he spoke over his shoulder to Max. "She fizzes up real easy."

"Like champagne." Max's tone was amused.

Lucy's hands fisted. "I have every right to be angry."

To her surprise, Max nodded. "I'm sorry you got in the middle of this. I had no intention of hurting or humiliating you, but I didn't have a choice."

Examining his words, she decided she'd been offered no more than a halfhearted apology, if that. "Don't you think you owe me an explanation?" she demanded. "Why are you after Joe?"

"Let's sit down," Ford suggested, gesturing toward the lounge and the three metal and canvas director chairs grouped around it.

Lucy hesitated, then shrugged. Why argue? She chose a canvas chair, Max sat in the one across from her. Ford jacked up the back of the lounge before dropping down onto it with a jolt, making the webbing creak alarmingly.

"You break it, you buy me a new one," she warned her brother.

He flashed her a brief grin, but didn't say anything. A silence fell. Lucy glanced from one man to the other, vowing not to be the first to speak. She'd already asked her question—let them, or, rather, Max, reply.

Deliberately looking away from the men, she saw the tabby sitting nearby, watching what was going on. The cat rose and sauntered toward the chairs. Since the tabby never came near Ford, Lucy expected her to jump onto her lap. Instead the cat paused beside Max's chair, then, without so much as sniffing his shoe, she leaped up and sat on his knee, staring raptly into those chilly blue eyes of his.

"Yes," he said, "I like you, too. I think you're a lovely creature."

Lucy blinked, not believing this grim-faced man could possibly be speaking to a cat. And so tenderly. He caught Lucy's gaze as he caressed the tabby under her chin and then stroked his hand slowly down the length of her back. As he did, a glow appeared in the depths of his eyes.

When she began to feel that glow reflected within her, began to imagine his fingers caressing her instead of the cat, Lucy tried to break the invisible contact, but could not.

"You want to start the story, Ryder?" Ford asked. "Or do you want me to?"

His voice broke the spell. Lucy looked away, realizing only then that she'd been holding her breath. The cat jumped down and began stalking a bird near the magnolia tree between the yards.

"It'll be simpler to go on calling him 'Joe Dooley,'" Max said, "so I will."

"But that's his name," Lucy protested.

"Let the man talk, Sis," Ford urged.

"I'm investigating a fraud case Dooley's involved in," Max went on, "and he knows it. Knows me. That's why he ran."

"No question of his guilt?" Ford asked.

He inquired so casually that Lucy was sure he already knew the answer but wanted her to hear it.

"No question."

The idea of Joe being mixed up in something so sordid as fraud made Lucy grimace, but, though the finality in Max's voice was convincing, she held out. "I thought no one was considered guilty until proven so in court," she said.

The glance Max and Ford exchanged with each other was so clearly a "what does she know—she's not a cop" look that Lucy sighed and confessed, "Okay, so I admit I don't understand why he ran if he isn't guilty."

Max leaned forward. "Dooley's dangerous. Notify your brother or me if he tries to contact you."

"Dangerous?" she echoed, in some surprise.

"He's desperate," Max said, "and desperate men are always dangerous. Be careful. Don't ever agree to see him alone."

He spoke so urgently she felt chilled. Obviously Max believed what he said.

"Ryder thinks Dooley's likely to return to Clover," Ford put in, "and if he does, chances are he may try to get in touch with you. You listen up, and do what

Ryder says. And keep your door locked days as well as nights. I want a promise.''

She had no reason to refuse. Actually, after what she'd been told about Joe, she didn't care to see him again anyway. "I promise," she told her brother.

"Good. One more thing. Sophie reminded me the wedding presents are at the Franklin place, and she was wondering what you planned to do about them. I think she'd like to help you sort through them. So if you want, I can pick the presents up and bring them here.''

Lucy didn't care if she never saw a single one of those presents again, but she realized that sooner or later someone would have to see about returning them. Obviously she would be that someone. Not now, though, not even with Sophie's help. She simply didn't feel like coping with the chore yet.

"Tell Sophie thanks, it's good of her to offer," she said. "But I'd rather wait. So just leave the presents where they are for the time being. They'll be safe at the mansion. I do have some of my belongings there that I'd like to pick up sometime soon, though. Maybe you could go with me.''

"You sure as hell better not go there alone. Come to think of it, this is Ryder's case, so he has an interest in the Franklin place." He turned to Max. "How about taking my sister out there to pick up her stuff?''

"Anytime," Max said.

Lucy didn't much care for the substitution, but knew it would do her no good to say so.

"You'll have no trouble contacting Ryder 'cause he'll be staying right next door," Ford said.

"To you?" she asked.

"No, to you. Polly's agreed to rent him her guest room. She says now that she's getting on, she likes the idea of having a cop in the house. Her father was one of Charleston's finest, you know."

"Yes, so she's told me. But Clover's got a hotel, three nearby motels, bed-and-breakfasts and Katie's place so why did Max—" She broke off and turned to Max as the answer came to her. "You're staying at Polly's so you can keep an eye on me, aren't you?"

"You're the bait," he agreed. "I'm the fisherman."

The idea didn't appeal to her. "Do you really think Joe will come here?"

"I know he will. Sooner or later."

"You'll be safer with Ryder close by," Ford said. "It'll be a load off my mind." His beeper went off, letting him know he had a call on his car radio. "See you later," he told them as he rose.

Lucy watched him go. "I imagine you're eager to get settled into Polly's," she said to Max, "so I won't keep you."

He made no move to leave. "I travel light."

Since Lucy found no response to that and Max didn't say anything more, the silence built up between them, not a friendly silence but one filled with tension. Finally she grew so uncomfortable that she blurted the first thing that came to her mind. "Do you always wear black?"

One corner of his mouth crooked up. "You've noticed."

He seemed addicted to dead-end responses. "I suppose if I ask you why you're so sure Joe's going to show up here I'll get another succinct, cryptic, unsatisfactory answer.''

He raised his left eyebrow, already slightly elevated by a scar, higher. "You should have warned me you preferred long, involved explanations."

"I can understand why Joe might return to the Franklin mansion," she said. "After all, he lived there and might need to retrieve things he needs—but I don't expect him to come to my cottage. What for?"

"To retrieve his bride. You."

Lucy stared at him. "Why would he think I'd go with him? He must know you've told me he's involved in a fraud case."

The curl of his lip wasn't one of amusement. "I've been told love is blind. And if it isn't in your case, that would make little difference to him."

Lucy blinked. "Do you mean you believe he'd force me to go with him?"

"'Force' is the key word here. At this point Dooley doesn't give a tinker's damn how you feel about him."

"But you can't *know* that."

Both his eyebrows raised. "Why not? I'm a longtime student of Dooley."

"Yet you claim that's not really his name."

"We'll stick to it for the time being."

"In other words you don't intend to tell me any more."

"Your brother said you were a quick study."

His sarcasm was the last straw. She jumped to her feet, glaring at him with her arms folded across her chest. "Are you always nasty or is there something about me you don't like?"

"Nasty?" he echoed, frowning.

"That's the word I used. I've tried to be civil to you. You could at least return the favor."

"Maybe I'm responding to the hostility behind your self-termed civility. Or it could be you're afraid of me, rather than hostile."

Taken aback, Lucy gathered herself to deny his accusation, then hesitated. She might not fear him, but he did unnerve her. "It's the way you keep assessing me with those ice blue eyes of yours," she confessed reluctantly. "As though you're tallying my faults."

Max broke into full-throated, genuine laughter. When he could speak, he said, "Sit down, Lucy, please do. So far I like everything about you except the fact I'm getting a crick in my neck looking up at you." When she eased back down onto the canvas seat, he added, "Can we start over?"

She nodded shortly, still unsure about him.

He leaned forward, extending his hand. "Hello, I'm Max Ryder, a suspicious man and slow to trust anyone."

Lucy hesitated, then, making up her mind, she leaned to put her hand in his, saying, "Hi. My name's Lucy Maguire." She flashed him a mischievous grin. "On second thought make that the faultless Ms. Maguire."

Amusement warmed his eyes as he grasped her hand, but as he continued to hold it firmly in his, the amusement gave way to an entirely different emotion, one that made her breath catch.

"Damn," he muttered, releasing her, "I was afraid of this."

He didn't have to explain, because she, too, had felt the indescribable current that flashed between them during their prolonged contact.

"Do you understand now why he's coming back for you?" Max asked.

She shook her head, not trusting her voice.

"Dooley felt it," Max told her.

"But I—" She stopped abruptly when she realized what she'd been about to admit. She might have no idea what to call the current that had passed between her and Max, but she knew absolutely she'd never felt such a thing before, never in her life, not with any other man—not even with Joe Dooley. But she certainly didn't intend to reveal that to Max.

His face softened, giving her a glimpse of a different side of him.

"Good."

He'd spoken so softly she'd barely heard the word.

He can't possibly know what I'm thinking, she assured herself. But if not, then what did he mean?

A moment later his face, if not as grim as before, came close to it. Rising, he said, "As you mentioned, I need to get settled in next door. We'll meet again."

She watched him stride across the lawn into her neighbor's yard, skirt Polly's house and disappear around the front. Meet again? She smiled wryly. That was a given, since she was the bait and he the fisherman, but she was far from being as certain as he was that the fish had any interest in the bait.

If Joe was as eager to reach her as Max seemed to believe, why hadn't he made any effort to contact her in the past two weeks? Max hadn't been in town during that time; he'd been off searching for Joe. If Joe had called or written her, then she could have used her own judgment about whether to notify Ford. But hearing Max's story had taken away that option, forcing her into the uncomfortable role of informer.

She wondered how long Max would camp in Polly's guest bedroom, waiting, before he gave up and returned to wherever he'd come from. Whether Joe stayed away or actually tried to visit her didn't change the fact that she had to pick up her belongings. She couldn't leave them at the mansion forever. This meant notifying Max so he could go with her. Lucy shook her head. Luckily there was no hurry; she had time to think about what she wanted to do.

While she'd promised her brother to be careful, she hadn't promised him to make Max her shadow.

Unfortunately, as she discovered in the next few days, no one had told Max he wasn't supposed to be her shadow. Every time she went into her backyard, he appeared in Polly's, and while he didn't actually walk her to and from work, he managed to show up at the library every day.

"Have you noticed that hunk in the black turtleneck?" Marian said to her on Thursday. "He must be new in town."

Knowing perfectly well the hunk was Max, Lucy marveled that Marian didn't recognize him as the man who'd chased Joe. "Um," she murmured, deliberately noncommittal.

That evening, she confronted him. "I see you skulking in Polly's grape arbor," she called to him from her backyard.

"I'm not skulking," Max countered, strolling toward her. "I'm merely looking for luna moths. Did you know they haunt vineyards? I learned that today in the library."

"If you don't quit following me everywhere, I may be fired."

"I haven't spoken one word to you at the library," he said, stopping beside her. "No one knows why I'm there. Besides, I think your boss is getting ready to come on to me." He grinned at her. "Think how disappointed she'd be if I failed to show."

"Marian is *not* coming on to you."

"Then why does she call me a hunk?"

"Eavesdropper!"

"That does happen to be one of my talents," he admitted, stooping to pick up the tabby, who was winding in and out between his ankles. "How about inviting Persephone and me in for coffee?"

"Persephone? That can't be her name—it's too hard to say. Anyway, I've never heard Polly call her anything but Kitty."

"Persy, then. She's very fond of you, so she won't mind the informality."

Lucy rolled her eyes. Somehow she'd allowed the conversation to get completely off the track, quite possibly because he'd confused her by being so casual and friendly.

"On second thought," he added, "if you have any leftovers, I think Persy might prefer some of the fish you had for dinner."

"Did you follow me to the fish market, too?"

He shook his head. "Smelled it cooking. Just coffee for me, though."

Giving up, she invited him in, refilled the coffeemaker and then placed a few scraps of fish on a plate she'd set on the floor for the tabby, who now seemed to be named Persy. While she got out the mugs, she planned what to say to Max. It was ridiculous for him to go everywhere she did. Even supposing Joe intended to kidnap her, which she sincerely doubted, he was hardly likely to do so in the library.

She poured coffee into Max's mug and set it on the tiny kitchen table in front of him. Carrying her own mug, she eased into a chair across from him. Now.

"Persy wants you to have one of her kittens," Max said before she could begin her speech. "She knows this will be her last litter, so she'll be upset if you don't agree."

Lucy stared at him. "Are you crazy?"

"Not that I've noticed. I'm merely reporting Persy's wish. Will you take a kitten or not?"

The tabby, she noticed, had finished the fish and was sitting at her feet, gazing up at her as if imploring her to listen to Max. "I was sort of planning to anyway," she admitted.

The cat jumped into Lucy's lap and, between purrs, began to clean her fur.

"So that's settled to everyone's satisfaction," Max said. She thought she detected a tinge of smugness in his tone.

"Persy may be satisfied," Lucy corrected, "but I'm not."

"Come to think of it, neither am I," he said.

Lucy blinked, uncertain where he meant to go from there but determined to get her complaint in first. "You simply must stop following me," she told him.

He sat up straighter. "That's not negotiable."

"I promise I'll let you or Ford know if Joe tries to get in touch with me, and you're right next door if he should show up at my house. You can't really imagine I'm in any danger in broad daylight here in Clover, so why—"

"Dooley's not going to phone or write you. He doesn't need to."

"I don't understand."

"You wouldn't even if I tried to explain, and I hope to God you never have to find out what I mean. Dooley's dangerous in ways you've been lucky enough not to experience. So far. I'm trying to keep it like that by sticking as close to you as I can."

The cat leaped to the floor, stalked to the door and meowed. Lucy got up and let her out. Standing by the door, she said, "I suppose you've shared all this with Ford, so that he knows exactly what you're talking about even if I don't." Anger spiced her words.

Max rose, crossed to her and gripped her shoulders, staring into her eyes. "I can't be more specific, either to your brother or to you, but I intend to do everything in my power to keep you from harm. From Dooley."

His words sent a worm of fear crawling through her, though she wasn't quite sure whether she was afraid of the unknown danger he refused to speak of or of Max himself.

"Is your front door locked?" he asked.

She bit her lip, aware she'd forgotten. "It's not dark yet," she equivocated.

Max dropped his hands from her shoulders, turned her about and marched her to the front of her cottage. "Dead bolts are no good unless you use them," he warned.

"Hardly anyone in Clover has dead bolts," she said, "but my brother insisted on putting them on both my doors when I moved in here."

"Ford's a smart man. Remember to lock the door every time you come in or leave the house."

When she finished with the front door, he led her to the back, saying, "When I go, lock this behind me." He glanced at the windows and sighed. "This is no fortress, that's for sure."

"I don't want to live in a fortress," she said, her voice showing her distress.

"I don't blame you."

Max cupped her face between his hands, making her heart race.

"I told you I wasn't satisfied, and I meant it," he said softly. "Since there isn't a damn thing I can do to change things, now or afterward, I know I never will be."

Bemused by the glow in his eyes, warmed by his touch, she didn't try to decipher what he meant. Nothing mattered but his nearness and the strong and vital current flowing between them.

"Oh, God, Lucy, I can't help myself," Max said huskily, and covered her mouth with his.

If this is what a kiss is supposed to be, she thought dazedly, then I've never been kissed before. Then her mind shut down as she spun into a realm of heat and passion, of desire and need. Whatever she could give him, she would, freely and eagerly. Whatever he gave her she would take with joy and then want more and more and more....

CHAPTER THREE

Okay, so he wasn't going to be able to sleep. Max cursed, rose from his bed in Polly Smith's guest room and padded to the window. The bed wasn't the reason he couldn't sleep. The bed, the mattress, the room were comfortable enough—very comfortable, in fact—but *he* sure as hell wasn't.

He stared down at the roof of Lucy's cottage, silvered by a gibbous moon. No light shone from any of her windows. Why should it at three in the morning? And why did he feel so edgy?

He glanced around his darkened room. He was alone. Though he couldn't see any of the pieces of the old-fashioned maple furniture clearly, he knew everything was exactly where it should be. Whatever was bothering him was not in this room.

As he turned back to the window, movement caught his eye and he tensed, focusing on the lawn. When he saw the rabbit hopping toward the cover of the azalea bushes next to Lucy's cottage, he relaxed. He hadn't really expected it to be anything dangerous, and because of his ability to sense Dooley's presence long before the bastard got close to him, he'd known it wasn't the man he'd stalked for five frustrating years.

Dooley wasn't the right name, but it would do well enough and had the advantage of being familiar to Ford and Lucy, as well as the rest of Clover. For all he knew, despite his research into the man's past, perhaps the name he'd discovered and had been using wasn't Dooley's real one, either.

Unfortunately, Dooley was almost as skilled at sensing aberrants as he was, one of the reasons he hadn't caught up to him sooner. He'd been working on ways to block his presence from Dooley and thought he might finally have succeeded. If he hadn't, Dooley would have skipped town long before Max got close enough to push open the doors of the church. This time Dooley had to see him to know he was there.

He watched Persy slip from the shadows under the magnolia and creep toward the bushes where the rabbit had taken shelter. Another hunter of the night after prey. But, unlike Dooley, the cat had an honest reason.

Since, like the cat, Max rarely made any move without a reason, he asked himself why he was standing at the window. What was he waiting for? His ability as an aberrant had driven him there, he was certain, but, as so often happened, the reason was still hidden from his conscious mind. Eventually he'd realize, but he was not a patient man.

He did comprehend why he hadn't slept. What perverse demon had led him to kiss Lucy Maguire? Alluring as she was, he'd known better, yet he hadn't been able to resist.

Even in the church, intent as he'd been on Dooley, he'd felt her bright sparkle as he'd pounded past her. It made him understand why Dooley wanted her, though it wasn't completely clear yet why he'd tried to marry her. Dooley had never bothered with marriage before.

Naturally enough, the same shining aura of Lucy's that had attracted Dooley had beckoned enticingly to him. He could feel her glow now, damped down by sleep but still a potent invitation. Too potent for his peace of mind. If he didn't need her to lure Dooley, he'd cut and run. His painful experiences with female aberrants had taught him a bitter lesson—stay clear or get hurt. Or at least he thought he'd learned that lesson. Evidently he was a fool for punishment.

Despite the awareness trouble lay ahead, he'd ignored all the danger signals and kissed her, the equivalent of pouring gasoline on an already raging fire. What he'd done was worse than stupid, it was positively suicidal. He'd broken his own rule of not getting involved with women like Lucy, and to add to the problem, he had no real idea how strong an influence Dooley might have over her.

What made it an even more devilish coil was that she understood little, if any, of this. He wasn't sure she knew what she was, and he'd lay odds she didn't realize how attuned she was to Dooley, or the terrible ways the man might use that attunement.

Basically he couldn't trust Lucy. She could betray him without being aware of what she was doing, could get him killed even against her will. Yet he didn't dare reveal any more than he'd already told her.

He couldn't be honest with her brother, either. The sheriff could be willing to help a PI tracking down a man for a defrauded client, but Ford wouldn't be able to accept the darker truth. Not that he'd told any lies. Dooley was certainly guilty of fraud, among worse crimes. What he'd done to Olivia—

No! Max took a deep breath, counting to ten as he let the air out slowly. He had to keep the past buried as deep under stone as Olivia was. Otherwise he'd fail to stay cool and Dooley would win. Again.

Focus on the present, Ryder, he warned himself. On Lucy. What do you know about her?

"Lucy changed after she met Dooley," her brother had told him. "He influenced everything she did. Some of it didn't matter, like her always wearing blue because he told her to. Or keeping her hair long and parted in the middle. I sort of like long hair myself. But when he began cutting her off from her friends..." Ford shook his head. "I didn't say anything 'cause Lucy already knew I wasn't crazy about Dooley and I didn't want to alienate her."

"He was trying to take her over," Max said, without thinking.

"You got the guy pretty well pegged," Ford had agreed. "I guess I was as annoyed at Lucy for letting him get away with it as I was angry at Dooley. It was as though she no longer had a mind of her own."

Ford didn't know the half of it, Max thought now, as he had at the time the sheriff had confided in him. Manipulating minds was bad enough, but it was far from the worst havoc Dooley could wreak.

From his window Max watched an owl drift on soundless wings over the cottage roof. Another hungry night hunter. He hoped Persy had the sense to remain undercover until the owl flew past, since the big birds considered cats as much their prey as any other small animal.

Hunters such as Dooley were more particular. Not every human would do, only those with something extra. Like Lucy. Like Olivia. Max clamped down on the surfacing memory—Olivia was beyond saving, but Lucy was still alive.

She hadn't been dressed all in blue when he'd met her in her backyard—he'd noticed her shirt was yellow. A sign she was trying to reject the spell Dooley had cast over her? She could if she knew how. Untutored as she was, though, she'd fail. He could teach her, given the right circumstances. Which he damn well didn't have.

To learn, she would first have to accept what she was. And he would have to put his desire for her on hold. Supposing they individually managed these two difficult tasks; there was no guarantee Dooley wouldn't step in before she was ready and mess everything up.

Max came alert, all his senses focused on the cottage as he picked up a sudden flare from Lucy. He relaxed slightly when she settled into her normal waking pattern. What, he wondered, had startled her into rousing? After a few minutes, the back door of the cottage opened and Lucy stepped into the night.

Sliding into his black jeans, he rammed his feet into moccasins, hurried downstairs and out Polly's back door. Moving as soundlessly as any other night hunter, he reached the cover of the magnolia and paused, watching her. Warily he extended his special sense, finding no immediate threat of danger.

Why had Lucy left the house? Was it on her own or because she'd been compelled to? She drifted about the yard from shadow to moonlight, enticingly lovely in a nightgown that didn't quite reach her knees, searching for something. What?

"Kitty?" she called softly. "Persy? Are you out here?"

He frowned. Why was she looking for the cat?

Persy emerged from the azalea bushes and, tail in the air, minced toward her. Lucy bent and scooped her up. "Thank heaven you're all right," she murmured, cuddling the tabby. "I dreamed a dog was chasing you, a huge black dog with red eyes."

Under the magnolia, Max clenched his jaw. Damn!

"But he didn't catch you, did he?" Lucy said to the cat.

"Not yet," Max said, stepping out from under the tree into the moonlight. "But who knows what might happen if you keep wandering about in the dark?"

Lucy's gasp of fright at his sudden appearance was followed by her angry "You!"

"Me," he agreed.

"And still in black, I see. You're probably the reason I dreamed of a black dog in the first place," she accused.

"You're wrong. The dream dog has nothing to do with me." As he spoke he tried not to notice the suggestive way the soft cotton gown clung to her.

Persy wriggled in her arms, twisting until she eased the cat onto the ground. When she straightened she snapped, "It's *my* dream, not yours."

"That's what worries me. I hope you don't intend to rush into the darkness every time a nightmare dog haunts your dreams."

She gathered herself as though for an indignant reply, then sighed. "It was a horrible dream—and so real. The dog—" She paused and hugged herself. "His red eyes were pure evil."

"The last time I looked in a mirror," he said, "my eyes were still blue. Look, Lucy, the night is too dangerous for you to be wandering around out here. Why don't you go back inside?"

She shook her head. "Not until I get rid of the tag ends of my nightmare. You don't understand how I felt—it was as though the dog were right there in my bedroom."

"I thought you said he was chasing Persy."

"He was."

"In your bedroom?"

"No, not in my house. Or any house. Somewhere else." She gestured vaguely.

"Do you remember any details of this somewhere else?"

"Not really. There was a fence, I think, but I'm not sure." She stared up at him, her eyes dark in the moonlight. "Why are you asking all these questions?"

"To help you get rid of the tag ends. Was the fence wooden? Iron? A stone wall?"

"Um, maybe iron, I don't really—" She broke off and shivered. "I just realized something. No wonder I'm so upset. *I* was Persy in that dream. I was the cat that devil dog chased."

"Yes," he said, "I think you were." He put his arm around her shoulders and urged her toward the house. "Come on, I'll go inside with you and stay until you feel calm enough to kick me out."

Instead of obeying, she turned to him and whispered, "Could you hold me for a minute? Just hold me?"

Lady, you don't know what you're risking, he thought as his arms closed around her.

He tried to concentrate on details in an effort to block his overwhelming urge to crush her to him and unleash his own devil of passion. The breeze, he realized for the first time, carried the scent of honeysuckle, its sweetness mingling with Lucy's inviting scent.

As his hands molded the cotton gown she wore to her soft curves, he fought against imagining how it would feel to caress her nakedness. He'd already sampled her lips, and struggled with his longing for another intoxicating taste, all the while knowing if he gave in it was possible neither of them would survive.

"I'll keep you safe," he murmured comfortingly, wishing he spoke the truth. She'd never be safe as long as Dooley lived. At the moment, he couldn't even promise she was safe from him.

She sighed and he felt her relax under his hands. Unable to help himself, he tightened his grip until she was snuggled close against him. No more than this, he vowed, feeling the exciting tingle of her aura mingling with his, a more potent aphrodisiac than any potion invented by man.

"This feels so right," she whispered, as if echoing his thoughts.

It *was* right. Right in a way she didn't yet understand, and therefore dangerous, as well. Dangerous as hell....

Savoring being held against the hard length of Max, Lucy realized that even in the midst of the most passionate kisses she and Joe had exchanged, she'd never felt the rightness of what they were doing. And she never would have, she was sure, even if she'd married Joe. Because she understood now that he was the wrong man.

Did that mean Max was the right one? Confusion dimmed her glowing pleasure, but she couldn't bring herself to pull away. Not yet, not when what she wanted more than anything else was to stay in Max's arms.

She and Max were barely acquainted, she knew hardly anything about him and what she knew held a distinct tinge of oddness, but that didn't matter. Should it matter? She was sailing into uncharted waters—it was almost as though the two of them were gloriously intermingling in some unusual, nonphysical way. Where would this lead? Would she be able to draw back, even if she wished to?

She'd thought that if he held her for a moment the dregs of her nightmare would vanish. She'd been correct. But hadn't she really wanted more? Hadn't she secretly longed for a repeat of the heady excitement that had rushed through her when he'd kissed her hours before? She'd certainly gotten more than she could ever have imagined.

How easy to give herself up to the wonder of the swirling flow between them and be carried beyond the boundaries of herself. At the same time, how frightening. Who was Max Ryder? What was he? A private investigator, yes, but what else? Why couldn't she resist him?

"Lucy," he murmured, "we have to stop before it's too late."

She nodded, agreeing intellectually but evidently in no other way, because she couldn't make herself pull free. Instead she found herself burning with her intense desire to kiss him.

"Lucy, sweet Lucy," he said hoarsely, both passion and desperation in his tone, "you must help me. The link is so strong I can't break it alone."

Gripped by her increasingly urgent need to have him kiss her, she struggled to ask, "How?" as she rose on her tiptoes, wrapped her arms around his neck and pulled his head down. Before he could answer, their lips met.

He tasted of a darkness that invited her into its secret mystery, a darkness she feared to enter, while at the same time she yearned for. His kiss, hot and insistent, tempted her beyond her will to resist.

She'd waited all her life for a man like Max, a man who would storm into her life and revitalize her world, a man who could take her to the heights by a mere touch of his hand. She should have had the sense to realize Joe had been nothing more than a substitute for the real thing.

Locked into their mutual passion, she offered herself wordlessly to Max in every way she could. Yes, she said with her lips, her tongue, her body. Yes, yes.

A voice coming from nowhere filled her consciousness, saying, *Not yet, child.* Somehow she knew the chiding words were her grandmother's. She tried to ignore them, but they continued to echo in her mind, growing louder and more insistent, until at last she heard the truth within them.

The time was not now. Accepting that truth gave her the strength to pull back, and she pushed her hands against his chest until he released her.

Max turned from her, raising his face to the moon while taking ragged, deep breaths. "Go inside, Lucy," he ordered when he could speak. "Go in and lock the door. Now!"

Not daring to look at her, he felt her leave, heard her open the door, close it behind her, before the dead bolt clicked faintly. Only then did he venture to relax his tight control.

He had never wanted a woman so much. Nor had he ever entered a linkage he couldn't break at will. It scared him to hell and gone. Lucy Maguire was danger personified. He had to keep his hands off her or he damn well wouldn't come out of this mess alive—and neither would she.

The only positive thing about their linkage was that he'd discovered Lucy was a virgin. Now he understood why Dooley had been forced to risk marriage to get his hands on her. Evidently she hadn't been willing to go to bed with him otherwise and Dooley hadn't dared take her by force, not with her brother the local sheriff and already leery of him.

He dropped onto the lounge chair, and almost immediately Persy arrived and curled up on his legs. As he absently stroked the purring cat, he remembered the black dog and grimaced. Bad news. Dooley wasn't near enough for him to sense, but Lucy's dream proved he couldn't be too many miles distant and that he was still determined to have her.

Max knew what the dream meant and where Dooley wanted her to go. She'd believed the fence was iron, and the grounds of the Franklin mansion were surrounded by an iron fence. Should he risk telling Lucy exactly what her dream was all about? He shook his head. She wouldn't believe him and so she'd still be in peril, but less likely to trust him. Still, the situation, though worrisome, wasn't hopeless.

What she must not do was to go to the mansion alone. Ford had delegated him to take Lucy there when she was ready to retrieve her belongings and with him along she would be safe enough because he could sense Dooley's presence. If Dooley was anywhere in the vicinity of the mansion, Max wouldn't let her go near the place. In the meantime, he would continue to visit the mansion daily to make sure Dooley hadn't returned to hole up there.

If Lucy dreamed again of the black dog, their linkage was now so strong that her terror would rouse him and send him hurrying to the cottage. Max nodded, as satisfied as he could be given the circumstances. Dooley would have a tough time if he tried to force Lucy to meet him at the mansion. Or anywhere else.

He glanced at the cottage and saw a lighted window in what he knew to be Lucy's bedroom. He couldn't blame her for leaving a lamp on and he'd be surprised if she was able to sleep. Between Dooley and him she had enough to disturb her sleep for a long time to come.

Lucy flung the magazine she'd brought to bed with her across the room. Why had she imagined she'd be able to concentrate enough to read after what had happened between her and Max?

"Were you really there, Grandma?" she whispered.

Impossible. But her grandmother's voice had been so clear....

Another strange item to add to her growing list, Lucy told herself unhappily. Ever since that vision she'd had of Dracula when she'd met Joe, there'd been one peculiar thing after another.

Her wedding had begun with a vision of her bouquet rotting, then Max had rushed into the church and Joe had fled from him, ending any chance of continuing the wedding. Before she'd left St. John's she'd had another inexplicable vision—of Luke Cassidy changing into another man.

Did her dream of the black dog count? She thought maybe it did. And certainly everything that had gone on between Max Ryder and her since he'd first touched her went on that list.

She tried not to remember how terrifyingly wonderful she had felt in his arms, bound to him by something intangible and yet real, aware she'd never be able to forget him. He'd seemed to be as helpless to break free as she had been, though he'd obviously wanted to, so she couldn't blame him for trapping her in something she didn't understand.

She might not blame him, but she could and did resent him. It was clear *he* understood what had happened to them, even if she didn't. Since he did understand, why had he gotten them into such a tangle? If her grandmother hadn't helped her... Lucy cut off speculation along that line. What-ifs would very likely lead her into reliving those indescribable moments in Max's arms.

There would be no more such entanglements with Max, thank you very much.

She resented the way Joe had deceived her, but at least he wasn't around to annoy her further, while Max would continue to be the shadow that went in and out with her. How frustrating.

Catching sight of her image in the mirror over the dressing table that had once been her grandmother's, she stared at the unattractive picture she made, frowning, her long hair tangled every which way.

"I hate my hair," she muttered, shoving strands from her face.

Through the partly open door of the closet she could see some of her clothes hanging on the rod, every garment blue, and she snapped, "I loathe, despise and detest blue!"

Joe had done this to her. Made her someone she wasn't, made her into a blue-garbed saintly image for some obscure purpose of his own. Why had she allowed him to? Lucy chewed on a strand of her hair, glowering at herself in the mirror.

"You did it to yourself," she told her mirror image. "Joe cajoled and suggested, but *you* did it."

What's done can be undone, she told herself. Redone. Made over. Changed into a person I can bear to look at in the mirror, a person I can smile at.

The idea made her smile then and there, but it faded when she realized no matter what she did, only her appearance would change. Inside she'd still be the same old Lucy, prone to errors of judgment. Shrugging, she eased down, dragging her pillow with her, and stretched out on the bed. At least the part of her people saw would be different. She reached to turn off the bedside lamp and stopped.

No. Tonight she wasn't brave enough to face the dark alone. Not with the black dog waiting for her to dream. Although she immediately wondered where that morbid thought had come from, at the same time she recognized the irrational truth in it. She was convinced the devil dog could and would visit her dreams again.

But not tonight, she decided. If I don't sleep, I won't dream.

Sooner or later she would have to sleep, but she refused to worry ahead. One night at a time was all she could think about. Since she didn't intend to sleep, she rose and, without turning on any other lights, padded into the kitchen.

Staring from the window over her sink into her backyard, she saw the moon was low, close to setting. She also noticed a dark bulk on her lounge chair and frowned, knowing it was Max. Shadowing her.

Or did he see it as guarding? Did he expect to keep the black dog from her dreams? She started to shake her head, then hesitated as it occurred to her he might be trying to do just that. It wouldn't be any weirder than everything else around her seemed to be getting. She watched him for a while and then padded back to her bedroom, oddly comforted.

Dropping onto her bed, she closed her eyes, telling herself it was safe to fall asleep because Max would hold the black dog at bay for the rest of this night, at least.

But that didn't mean she'd changed her mind about him. He was an enigma she didn't care to waste time trying to understand. Or, to be exact, she was afraid of trying to understand. What if she were drawn into his strangeness and became irrevocably changed? One man had already done his best to alter her for his own purposes. She wasn't about to make the same mistake with another.

She'd begun to drift off, when her eyes popped open and she sat bolt upright as a question invaded her mind. When she'd accused Max of bringing the black dog to her dreams because of his penchant for wearing black, she'd only been partly serious. He'd easily convinced her she was wrong, and she probably had been. But what about all the other things she'd let him convince her of?

Ford had claimed he'd checked Max out and that he really was a licensed PI, so that part was true. But how much had he told her brother about this so-called fraud Joe was supposed to be guilty of? Enough so Ford could check the truth of it? Or had Ford simply accepted the story once he was sure Max was a private detective?

What if the entire tale, except for Max's profession, was a fabrication, a story told by Max to cover the real reason he was after Joe? That raised the possibility Joe wasn't guilty of fraud but feared Max for some reason that had nothing to do with criminal activity on his part, feared for his life, maybe, to the point where he'd run. If Joe *was* innocent, he had the right to present his side of the case.

Max had so bemused her with his near-hypnotic presence and his mind-altering kisses that she had dumbly accepted what he'd told her. There was a good chance she'd been made a fool of.

Ford had believed Max's word that she was in danger from Joe, but was she really? Joe had never tried to hurt her, why would he now? For some reason Max wanted to keep her away from any contact with Joe. Why? Was it for his own purposes? And what might those purposes be? Instead of her, was it really Joe who was in the most danger?

She couldn't answer the questions she'd posed, but she arrived at one tentative conclusion: she wasn't being fair to Joe. If she condemned him without giving him a chance to talk to her, she would be guilty of disloyalty to the man she'd promised to marry.

CHAPTER FOUR

Jeannie Potts stared at Lucy, her long, dark false eyelashes giving her an expression of exaggerated surprise. "You want *all* your hair cut off?"

"Not quite all," Lucy corrected, aware the other patrons in the beauty shop were avidly listening. "Just most. I want my hair short and curly."

Jeannie lifted a strand of Lucy's long hair, examined it and shook her head. "Such thick, healthy hair. I've got customers who'd trade their back teeth for hair like this. Sure you won't change your mind? I could give you a real nice perm with it long, you know."

"Short," Lucy said firmly. It had taken her days to make up her mind what she wanted and she was determined to stick to her decision.

Jeannie shrugged. "The customer's always right, that's what I say. And hey, if you do find you made a mistake, the nice thing about hair is it always grows back. Sort of like giving you a second chance."

Lucy nodded. Second chance? For her hair, maybe, but certainly not for Max Ryder. He'd get no second chance from her. He was still shadowing her, if more discreetly, but she hadn't actually seen him to speak to since that night she'd dreamed about the black dog. The dream, thank heaven, had not returned, and Max also had refrained from seeking her company. Which was exactly the way she wanted it.

She was relieved when the three other customers in the shop lost interest in her and resumed talking or reading a magazine. Two were older, Sadie Byrans and Zenia Moxley. Mina Martin, about Lucy's age, was sitting across from Edie, the manicurist, who came in twice a week to do nails for Jeannie's clientele. Edie, Lucy saw, was replacing one of Mina's long, silver stick-on nails.

"You ever hear from Joe?" Jeannie asked, speaking for once in a low tone.

Lucy shook her head.

"A shame something like that had to happen," the hairdresser continued, her voice regaining its normal volume, so everyone in the shop heard her. "I've noticed that guy around town a couple of times—the one who chased Joe, I mean. Hear he's renting a room at Polly Smith's. You ever see him?"

Again Lucy shook her head. After all, it was more or less true, at least lately.

"Well, I can't blame you for not wanting to have anything to do with him. Or any other male right now. Even if he is a hunk. Right?"

Lucy didn't reply.

"Believe me, he *is* a hunk," Mina announced. "His name's Max Ryder and we had lunch together at the diner the day before yesterday. Peg's special fried chicken." She pursed her lips. "Mmm. And I don't mean the food."

Every woman in the place focused on Mina.

"So, you going out with him again?" Jeannie asked.

Mina shrugged. "Maybe I will and maybe I won't."

"In my day, that meant he hasn't asked you yet," Zenia put in.

Mina's brown eyes narrowed and she tossed back her auburn mane. "He said he'd call, but I have better things to do than wait around for the phone to ring. The fact is, we got along like a house afire, if you know what I mean. He'll be back for more."

"Don't move your hand or the nail won't stick on right," Edie warned Mina, who then returned her attention to the manicurist.

Lucy assessed Mina in the mirror. She *was* pretty, with her pale skin, dark-red hair and brown eyes, no doubt about that. If she wore clothes that left little to the imagination, they did show off a very good figure. Mina never had any difficulty attracting men, but she seemed to tire of them quickly.

As though she sensed Lucy's regard, Mina said over her shoulder, "I haven't had a chance to say I was sorry about what happened to your wedding, Lucy. I mean, it isn't the kind of thing you send a condolence card for, and I didn't want to bother you by calling or anything like that. I hope you're doing okay."

Lucy was tempted to intone solemnly, "The bereaved is holding up as well as can be expected," but quelled her wayward impulse and merely smiled. After all, Mina meant well.

If Max was interested in Mina, she didn't care one bit. Not at all. It was none of her affair what he chose to do or with whom he chose to do it.

"Hope you don't mind me asking," Jeannie said to Lucy, "but did you ever find out why this Max Ryder was after Joe?"

"Perhaps he told Mina," Lucy said, sidestepping the question.

Mina turned to face her. "That's not the kind of thing we talked about," she said.

"He must have told you something about himself," Jeannie said.

Mina shrugged. "Can I help it if he was more interested in finding out about me than he was in giving me his life history?"

"In other words, you did all the talking and he never got a word in edgewise," Zenia said. "No wonder he didn't ask you to go out with him again."

Mina glared at Zenia. "If I decide I want Max Ryder, I can have him. Like that." She snapped her fingers, her silver nails gleaming.

And welcome to him, Lucy told herself, ignoring the empty feeling in the pit of her stomach.

For a few minutes no one spoke. There was only the snip-snip of the scissors shearing off Lucy's dark hair, the sound of the dryer Sadie sat under and, very faintly, rock music from Jeannie's radio, turned low because her older customers objected to her musical taste.

Finally Jeannie said, "What's your brother say about you cutting your hair short?"

Lucy raised her eyebrows. "Ford? I didn't ask. Why should I?"

"I don't know, I just thought maybe you would, he being your only family and looking after you for so long. I mean he was always so particular about who you dated."

"Scared most of them off," Zenia put in. "Didn't think anyone was good enough for his little sister."

"Until Joe Dooley came along," Jeannie said.

"Came and went," Zenia countered. "In my opinion, you're better off, Lucy. Letitia Franklin was as peculiar as they come."

"She was also the wealthiest woman in Clover," Mina commented. "Lucy would've been positively rolling in green stuff. Plus Joe was drop-dead gorgeous." She looked at Lucy. "Do you think he'll ever come back?"

"I suppose that depends on Max Ryder." Though Lucy had managed to speak calmly, her tone was tinged with bitterness.

"If Joe does come back he'll hardly know you with your hair all cut off and curled," Jeannie said. "I don't think you've ever had a perm—at least, I never gave you one."

To Lucy's relief, that brought a general discussion of straight versus curly and long versus short and what men liked and didn't like about a woman's hair. She was off the hook, thank heaven.

When all the curling and the rinsing and the neutralizing was over and Jeannie had blow-dried the end result, Lucy stared at her reflection in the mirror.

"What's the verdict?" Jeannie asked.

"I look—different."

"You'll get used to it. Sometimes it takes a while. I've had customers tell me they went home and cried over losing their long hair. But I noticed not a one of them grew it back real long ever again."

Lucy remembered having promised herself to smile at her new image. "I like it fine, Jeannie," she said. "It's exactly what I wanted, short and curly."

Later, in the PeeDee Boutique, she gathered clothes off the racks to try on, choosing any color but blue, finally buying three new tops, a pair of shorts, two dresses and a pair of dressy pants, all she could afford at the moment.

When she got home, she changed into a red top and white shorts, brushed through her hair until it fluffed around her face and smiled at the new Lucy, different from the skin out.

Her head felt pleasantly lighter without the long hair and the bright red of the top lifted her spirits. "So much for you, Joe Dooley," she muttered. If he ever returned she might listen to his side of the story because she owed him that much, but she didn't intend to take him back. Lucy Maguire was offering no second chances.

As for Max Ryder, she planned to ignore him.

The Bible might warn that some women were a snare and a delusion, but she'd learned that the cautionary words could apply to some men, as well.

That evening, after undressing for bed, she started to pull on her nightgown, only to hear an ominous ripping sound. When she examined the gown she shook her head. With such a huge tear, it was good only for the ragbag. Unfortunately the only other nightwear she had in the cottage was in the dirty-clothes hamper.

Her two best nightgowns were in the luggage that she'd left at the mansion. After the reception at the White Dolphin Inn, she'd intended to return to the mansion with Joe and change from her wedding dress before they went off on their honeymoon. He hadn't told her their destination, claiming he wanted to surprise her.

She smiled wryly. Surprise her he certainly had, though not in the way he'd planned.

As for the luggage, she needed to retrieve it. She'd gotten along with her older clothes up until now, but it was foolish to have all her best things out of reach, even if they were mostly blue. What was she waiting for anyway? For Joe to return so they could pick up where they'd left off?

Lucy shook her head. The truth was she didn't like the old Franklin place. Something about it troubled and depressed her, though she'd never admitted this to Joe. But, since she didn't have to go there alone, there was no reason to delay any longer.

And then she remembered who was supposed to accompany her. She'd hoped Sophie might go with her, but she knew Ford would have a fit if she asked his wife, plus Sophie probably wouldn't want to go anyway. Not with nobody knowing where Joe was or exactly what he was guilty of. Ford had delegated Max, and as far as her brother was concerned, Max it would be.

If he wasn't too busy with Mina.

Lucy really didn't want to ask Max to go with her. On the other hand, she didn't want to go alone, either. She wasn't a coward, but she found the Franklin mansion daunting in a way she didn't understand.

Bite the bullet, she told herself, and face being with Max. It won't be for very long, after all.

She rummaged in her dresser drawer for something to wear to bed and came up with an old T-shirt with a faded Charleston Rainbows logo from the days when she'd dated one of the players on the baseball team. She grimaced, recalling how quickly Ford had quashed that.

"The guy has a wife back in California," her brother had told her after investigating. "And if that's not enough to convince you, check out his RBIs—he'll never make the majors."

As she slid on the oversize T-shirt, she realized she could no longer clearly recall what the Rainbow shortstop had looked like. Would Joe's image someday fade and vanish from her memory? She closed her eyes and tried to picture him, but evidently pushed the wrong button, because it was Max's face that she saw, instead.

Though she did her best to dismiss Max's image from her mind, when she fell asleep he crept into her dreams, shadowing her even there....

Lucy, in the shape of a cat, perched in the magnolia tree between her yard and Polly's. On the limb next to her Persy crouched, both of them watching Max as he slowly circled Lucy's house clockwise, chanting and strewing fragments of dried plants behind him.

"What's he doing?" Lucy asked as Max disappeared from sight around the front of her cottage.

"Forming a protective circle to keep Shuck out," Persy replied.

"Who's Shuck?"

Persy's green eyes bored into her. "You know, you've met him."

Lucy blinked. "I don't remember."

"You will." Persy flicked her long, striped tail. *"No more questions about Shuck—I don't like to talk about him."*

"Up until now I didn't even know you could talk."

"You weren't listening with your inner ear. You didn't understand me and so I had to tell Max about my last kitten. I know she'll have a good home with you."

"I promise," Lucy said.

Max reappeared, coming around the far side of the cottage, veering to include the magnolia tree inside the protective circle he fashioned.

"We're safe for now," Persy said.

"Safe," Max echoed from beneath the tree. *"As safe as I can make you...."*

Lucy awoke in the morning remembering his words. But, of course, it was only a dream. Strange how she'd been a cat in two dreams now. Marian, at the library, would be sure to tell her it was symbolic—but what of?

The day was overcast, but the sky looked as though it might clear. She hoped so, because she hated to have it rain on the days she didn't have to work. Lucy donned her white shorts and red top again and went to the kitchen. While she was waiting for the coffee to drip through, she thought she heard the sound of a push mower. Opening the kitchen door, she glanced to her right and saw Max, still in black, mowing Polly's back lawn.

As though he'd been waiting for this cue, Max stopped, looked her way and waved. "Do I smell coffee?" he called.

"Come over and have some," she offered, telling herself the invitation was only because she needed to ask him about going to the Franklin mansion.

"I see you opted for the temporal rather than the saintly," he said, his gaze traveling over her as he accepted a mug of coffee. "I like the result."

Lucy resisted the impulse to run a hand through her curls. "Thank you." She took a sip of her coffee before saying, "If it's convenient for you, I'd like to pick up my things from the mansion today—not the presents, just my belongings."

"My time is your time."

"I don't want to interfere with your private life," she said, "so why don't you set the time."

He raised his eyebrows. "Private life? What private life?"

"Well, I mean, you must have met a few people around town by now."

"Just what are we talking about here?"

Feeling herself flush with a combination of embarrassment and annoyance, Lucy set down her mug with a thump. "It's not important. I was merely trying not to inconvenience you."

He eyed her assessingly, seemed about to speak and then shook his head. "Now," he said finally. "If we go now we can stop on the way for breakfast at Peg's Diner."

"No!" The word burst from her before she thought.

"You don't want to be seen in public with me—is that it?"

She fastened onto his words with relief, using them in place of her real reason. "I don't wish to feed the gossip mill and that's what would happen."

"In that case, I imagine it's all over town that I had lunch in the diner with a beautiful redhead named Mina."

None of the comments that came to Lucy sounded right. *Oh, really?* sounded as false as it was and *Yes, she is attractive,* wouldn't do, either. *I hope you enjoyed yourself* would make him think she cared what he did. She finally simply nodded.

"Mina was a gold mine of information," he said.

"I can imagine." Despite her best intentions, sarcasm tinged her voice.

Either missing or ignoring the sarcasm, he said, "Pretty women who are aware of their attractiveness are apt to be fairly candid about everyone except themselves. I saw the Clover folk I'm most interested in from Mina's point of view. Most enlightening."

Was he trying to convince her that his only reason for seeking Mina's company was to learn more about the people of Clover? He'd have to do better than that! Instead of responding, she returned to the subject that had begun this flight of fancy. "I'm ready to go," she said. "Never mind breakfast."

"Toast," he said.

"You want toast?"

"We want toast," he corrected. "You and I. First. Then we'll go."

Complying was easier than arguing, and besides, she *was* a tad hungry.

Later, seated in the passenger seat of Max's rental car, she tried not to imagine that everyone was peering curiously at her as they drove through Clover to reach Highgate Road. He'd insisted on taking his car, claiming it was larger and a lot newer than her rather elderly subcompact—facts she couldn't deny.

"Relax," he said, as if sensing her unease. "Most of them won't recognize the new Lucy anyway." He reached over and ran his fingers through her curls. "A tempting hairdo. I've been wanting to do that ever since I saw you come home yesterday."

She stared at him, nonplussed. "Tempting" was the last thing she'd had in mind when she'd told Jeannie to cut her hair. And she'd had no idea he was watching her yesterday. But what bothered her the most was how much she enjoyed the feel of his hand in her hair.

I shouldn't have touched her, Max told himself, keeping his gaze firmly away from the inviting expanse of legs revealed by her white shorts. He'd acted impulsively and he couldn't afford to. Not around Lucy.

While he applauded the statement she was making to one and all by changing her appearance to suit herself, he hadn't expected to be even more drawn to the new Lucy than he had to the old one.

"I had an odd dream last night," she said.

He tensed, waiting.

"You were circling my house," she went on, "with some kind of magic circle, or so Persy said."

He'd feared she'd dreamed of the black dog, but she'd surprised him. Smiling one-sidedly, he asked, "How do you know it was a dream?"

"Because I was a cat, up in the magnolia tree with Persy." She slanted him a triumphant look.

"Have it your way."

"It was a dream. Why do you always twist things?"

He shrugged. "What else did Persy tell you?"

"About her kitten. And—" Lucy frowned as if trying to remember. "And someone named Shuck. You were protecting my house against Shuck."

He controlled his dismayed reaction, merely repeating, "Shuck?"

"I think that's right. Persy wouldn't tell me who he is." She glanced at Max again. "You seem awfully interested in my dream. Usually people are bored to death when you try to relate a dream."

"I'm glad it wasn't a nightmare," he said, replying indirectly.

Damn. Somehow the bastard was getting through to her despite the blocks Max had set in his path. Dooley had found enough of a chink in the protective barriers to send a fragment of his message. Which meant he must be near Clover.

All senses alert, Max turned onto Highgate Road.

"You look grim again," Lucy observed. "The way you did in the church when you chased Joe."

"I think he's fairly close. Dooley, I mean."

Lucy drew in her breath. "At the mansion?"

"Not in it, not that close. I go by every day to check, and he hasn't returned there. Ford's keeping his eye out for him, too."

"Joe hasn't called me."

Lucy sounded as though she hoped he wouldn't, whether this was true or not. Max had no intention of telling her that he knew Joe hadn't phoned, because when her brother had had the Caller ID installed in her house, he'd also arranged for her phone to be tapped. Max had learned the hard way not to trust anyone.

"Where is your luggage?" he asked. He'd never been inside the mansion; he hadn't needed to go in to tell whether Dooley was there.

"One large blue floral patterned bag in the entry and maybe a matching small carryon, too. I'm not real sure about the carryon."

As the tall wrought-iron fence surrounding the grounds came into view, Max's uneasy sensation that Dooley was nearby increased. "I don't like this," he muttered. "I should have come out here alone."

"But I have the keys," she reminded him.

He gave her a tight smile, all he could manage at the moment. "Wouldn't you have given the keys to me if I'd asked you nicely?"

Lucy bit her lip. "I feel this is my responsibility."

"Is that a no?"

"More like an I don't know."

Max swung the car off Highgate Road and stopped in front of the iron gates. Wordlessly Lucy pulled a large iron key from her bag and handed it to him. After unlocking and throwing open the gates, Max returned to the car and gave back the key to Lucy, and they drove along the drive that twisted up a low hill planted with shrubs that had been allowed to run wild.

Southern pines clustered thickly around the three-story brick mansion, hiding all but its round, peaked tower from view. Atop the tower, a full-rigged ship decorated the iron weather vane.

"The early Franklins must have been seafarers," Max observed.

"I don't know. Joe hardly ever spoke of the Franklins."

Max wasn't surprised. Dooley was no fool; he knew it was better not to say anything than to make up stories and then be forced to remember your own falsehoods so you wouldn't be tripped up.

His sense of Dooley's presence didn't grow any stronger as they neared the mansion, convincing him that it was safe enough to enter, though not to linger. He would grab her luggage and get the hell away from the place.

"So this is where you were going to live," he said as he pulled up in front of the brick mansion.

"I said I would," Lucy told him uncertainly, "but I really didn't want to."

Curved brick steps with iron railings rose to a roofed entryway. The massive oak front door was set with two high, round windows, so that the house itself seemed to stare at those who climbed its steps.

"My things should be just inside the door," Lucy said as she slid from the car, a small brass key in her hand.

Beside her, Max nodded and held out his hand for the key, but she shook her head. He mounted the steps with her and waited while she inserted the key into an ordinary lock.

"Evidently the Franklins didn't worry about intruders," he said.

"Old Miss Letitia wasn't afraid of anything," Lucy said, "but at least half the town was leery of her."

"To quote Mina, Miss Letitia was 'really weird.'"

"Eccentric, anyway. She spoke to people no one else could see or hear. But she wasn't senile."

Lucy inserted the key in the lock and turned it, then hesitated so long that Max asked, "Having trouble?"

Without replying, she pushed open the front door.

The only natural light in the entry hall came through the small, round windows in the door and so they stepped into gloom. Lucy reached for the light switch, but Max shook his head.

"Don't bother," he said. "I see your bag. At least the larger one. Did you say there was a matching carryon?"

"I remember Joe mentioning that he was going to put the carryon in his car. I'm not sure if he did or not."

Hefting her bag, Max said, "The carryon's not here, and Dooley took off with the car, so only he knows for sure. Your brother put a call out for the car's license number, but apparently no one's spotted it yet." He nodded toward the door. "Let's go."

Lucy was only too glad to agree. The farther she was from the mansion, the better she liked it. As she was unlocking the front door, she'd had the strangest feeling that Joe was calling her. Not out loud, but in her head. Before she could be sure she wasn't imagining it, the sensation faded and disappeared.

On the way there, she'd told herself she ought to check on the wedding presents that had been stacked on the dining room table the last she saw them. But her experience before they entered, combined with the gloom of the entry hall, unnerved her, and she closed and locked the door behind her with a sense of relief.

Neither she nor Max spoke on the way back. He was pulling up in front of her cottage, when she recalled that she'd left, in an upstairs bedroom of the mansion, the blue silk suit she'd planned to wear after she'd changed from her wedding dress. And at the last minute, hadn't she taken the carryon up to that bedroom, as well? Maybe it wasn't in Joe's car after all. Should she ask Max to go back so they could take a look for the carryon while they retrieved the suit?

Lucy shook her head. She'd had enough of the Franklin mansion for one day. The big bag held what she needed the most—her other belongings could wait. Max's comment about her planning to live in the mansion had shaken her more than she'd let on. It was hard to believe that if Max hadn't appeared at the church when he had she *would* be living there at this very moment. With her husband. With Joe Dooley.

She no longer could imagine being Joe's wife. Or even that she'd agreed to be.

Max set her bag down in her living room. "How do you feel about all that's happened?" he asked, again uncannily aware of her thoughts. "Saved or sorry?"

CHAPTER FIVE

Saved or sorry? Max's words stuck unpleasantly in Lucy's mind like a bad taste left from something inedible. He had no right to ask her such a question. Feeling trapped, even though she was in her own living room, she glared at him.

"What business is it of yours?" she demanded.

"I don't care to be unexpectedly sabotaged," he told her. "Are you for Dooley or for me?"

"I'm neutral," she snapped.

He shook his head. "That's one position you can't hold for long. Not when the war heats up. And it will."

"War? You're not making sense."

"I'm on one side—Dooley's on the other. We're enemies."

"That doesn't mean *I* have to take sides."

"You're not a disinterested bystander, Lucy. You're smack-dab in the middle."

"I don't see what I have to do with a fraud case."

"Haven't you realized by now this is about more than the fraud Dooley's guilty of?"

"The fraud you say he's guilty of." Defiance sharpened her words. "How do I know you're telling the truth?"

"You don't."

She'd expected him to defend his position, and because he didn't, it took her a moment or two to regroup.

"Either you believe Dooley ran when he saw me because he's guilty," Max went on, "or you believe he ran because he's an innocent lamb and I'm the big bad wolf."

Lucy had come up against this problem in her own mind before and found no solution. Why *had* Joe run?

"While you think about it," he said, "I've got a lawn to mow."

After Max left, she carried her bag into her bedroom, doing her best to dismiss Max's image of lambs and wolves. And dismiss him, as well. She began unpacking and discovered only one of her nightgowns inside the bag. The other, she remembered belatedly, was in the carryon—either upstairs in the mansion or in Joe's car, wherever that was.

Max had said Joe wasn't far from Clover. How did he know? And if he knew where Joe was, why didn't he go after him? He seemed to hide more than he revealed.

She unpacked and stacked some of her things on top of her dresser. Once she'd hung up the clothes that belonged in the closet, she started putting the items on the dresser in their proper places. Before she finished, the blue velvet jewelry case caught her eye. She knew what was inside.

The case hadn't come from her bag. It had been sitting on the dresser since the day of her wedding because she hadn't cared to touch Joe's bridal gift. She didn't want to keep the necklace, but how was she supposed to return it to Joe?

Lucy sighed. If she'd planned ahead, she could have taken the diamond-and-sapphire necklace with her today and left it at the mansion. Unfortunately, the thought hadn't crossed her mind until this moment. She'd have to decide what to do with the necklace; she couldn't put it off much longer.

Sometime or other, she would also have to unroll the balled-up wedding underwear she'd shoved into her closet, wash the stuff and stash it—no, give it—away. The less around to remind her of her aborted wedding, the better. Something would have to be done with the wedding gown, as well.

Not now, Lucy told herself. That kind of thing is for a rainy day. Today is for being outside. For yard work. For mowing. The grass badly needs cutting.

In the past, her brother had often brought his power mower over and cut her lawn, but since Ford and Sophie had gotten married, she didn't see as much of him. Not that she minded. Much as she loved her brother, he still had this aggravating tendency to try to run her life as though she were seventeen instead of twenty-seven. She was as capable of managing her own affairs as she was of mowing her own lawn.

She was glad to see that Max was nowhere in sight when she walked across her backyard to the shed where she kept her push mower. As she entered the ramshackle shed, Persy jumped out of a box of odds and ends stored there and purred around her ankles. Noticing the cat's increasing girth, Lucy shook her head.

"Scouting the territory, are you? I told you this isn't a good place for your kittens—you know perfectly well the roof leaks. Look at the walls—full of cracks and holes. You probably sneaked in here through one of those holes. Why can't you use the nice nest that Polly fixed for you inside your house to kitten in?''

Persy followed her as she dragged the mower from the shed. The tabby leaped onto the lounge and watched through half-closed eyes as Lucy set to work.

Pushing the mower up and down the lawn, Lucy went over what she and Max had discussed while driving to and from the mansion. Did he suppose that she believed he'd taken Mina to lunch just to get her opinion of the folks in Clover? Fat chance. Max was an acute observer. He couldn't help but have noticed the three or four old men who hung out daily on the benches in the small park near the library. Surely he realized any one of them could have dredged up town gossip from the 1920s on, providing him with all he wanted to know—and more.

But, no, he'd chosen Mina, who, among other things, had told him Miss Letitia was weird. What, Lucy wondered, had Mina said about her? Not that it mattered. She didn't care one way or the other what Max thought of her.

Saved or sorry? Okay, so it was a relief not to be faced with living in the mansion. And she had to admit that the thought of making love with Joe now made her cringe. She blamed Max for her change of heart.

Had Max kissed Mina the way he'd kissed her? Grimacing, she gave the mower a savage shove, muttering "You can't trust men" to Persy as she passed the lounge.

Lucy saw no sign of Max for the rest of the day, and in the early evening, he drove off in his car. She resolutely refused to speculate on where he was going or with whom. Later she watched an old movie on TV until she was tired enough to go to bed.

As she checked to see if she'd locked the back door, she heard something scratch against the screen and, listening, caught Persy's meow. Surprised, she let the cat in. Though Persy had been in her house more than once, she'd never before scratched at the screen at night.

Persy wove around her ankles, then followed her into the bedroom, jumping heavily onto the bed. Lucy ran her hand over the tabby, who didn't seem in any distress or in any danger of dropping her kittens early.

"Checking out my bed, are you?" Lucy asked. "The bed's comfy and you're welcome to try it—but I'd prefer you choose another spot to have your babies when the time comes."

Persy closed her eyes and purred.

Wondering why the cat had decided to spend the night on her bed—a first—Lucy eventually settled in next to her and switched off the bedside lamp. "Good night Persy," she murmured. "Chase away any bad dreams, okay?"

It was, she realized as she drifted off, comforting to have the tabby with her. . . .

Lucy stood by her kitchen window, staring into the night. The moon was up, full and bright, showing her that nothing was out of place in her backyard. Even the glowing line across the grass belonged there. Invisible by daylight, it was part of Max's protective circle around the cottage, keeping her safe.

Her gaze sharpened, fixing on a spot just beyond the line, where a black mist was gathering. As she watched, the mist began to coalesce into a malignant form of darkness. The hair rose on her nape and she took two steps back from the widow.

What was that horrible creature in her backyard? As it solidified, she drew in her breath, suddenly aware she was looking at the black devil dog from her nightmare. The monster paced back and forth along the line, his eyes fiery red as he stared at her window.

Even though she'd stepped back, he knew she was there. His mouth opened in a savage snarl and the moonlight gleamed on sharp white teeth. She hugged herself, shivering. Was she safe from the beast? But even if Max's protective circle failed, surely the black dog couldn't pass through locked doors.

Doors, no. What about windows, though?

She drew in a gasping breath as she pictured the beast crashing through a window, shattering the glass as he plunged inside to—to what? Leap at her throat? No, that wasn't right. He hadn't come to kill her; he'd been sent for another purpose. To fetch her.

Where? To whom? What kind of monstrous master had devil dogs at his beck and call?

To her fearful dismay, she saw that the part of the circle where the black dog paced back and forth had begun to lose its glow. A hissing filled her ears, growing louder and louder, a hissing that didn't come from the dog. She knew if she focused on the sound the hissing would become a word and she would understand—what?

Concentrating, she tried to form a word. Sh—Sh— Shuck. It didn't make sense.

The line's glow gradually faded, darkening, turning as black as the devil dog. He lunged toward the *cottage. Toward her. Terror gripped her by the throat, cutting off her scream.*

"Shuck!" a man's voice shouted. "Begone Shuck!" The voice trailed off into gibberish that turned into hissing....

Lucy awoke abruptly, frozen with fear and feeling a weight on her chest. In the nightmare-induced fright combined with darkness, she didn't understand at first that Persy was standing on top of her, hissing. When she did, she pushed the cat aside, sat up and turned on the bedside lamp. The only thing to be seen was the tabby, her fur on end, spitting at nothing.

Someone—something?—began pounding on her back door. Did she hear her name being called? Forcing herself to her feet, she crept toward the kitchen, turning on lights as she went. When she reached the kitchen she heard, through the pounding, Max calling to her.

"Lucy! It's Max. Open up!"

Was it really him?

Persy, her fur back in place, trotted past her to the kitchen door and stood there waiting for Lucy to open it.

Easing close to the door, Lucy asked, "Max?"

"Yes," he said. "Let me in."

He sounded like Max and obviously Persy believed he was. Lucy flipped on the back light, turned the night lock, then the key that unlocked the dead bolt, and inched the door open. The man standing there in moccasins, black jeans and no shirt was unmistakably Max. Persy slipped through the opening and vanished into the night.

"The cat!" Lucy cried.

"She'll be safe enough," Max assured her, stepping into the kitchen. "Shuck won't be back tonight."

She clutched his arm. "But it was a dream. Wasn't it? A horrible, horrible dream."

Putting an arm around her, he led her toward her bedroom. "No more talking until you put on a robe. Otherwise, with that sheer nightgown you're wearing, I won't be able to keep my mind or hands from wandering."

As she slipped on a short cotton robe, she noticed Max looking around her bedroom as if searching for something.

But all he said was "Let's have some coffee."

Shards of the nightmare clung to Lucy as she automatically put a new filter in the coffeemaker, measured coffee, poured water in and turned it on.

"Sit down," Max ordered. "I'll get the mugs."

Not until they both sat at the kitchen table with filled mugs did he say another word. "Keep an open mind," he told her. "Don't discount what you hear merely because it goes against what you've been led to believe is true."

She gazed at him without understanding what he was getting at, but replied, "I'll try."

"You dreamed Shuck came," he said. "He did."

"Shuck." She repeated the word with distaste. "He's the black dog?"

Max nodded. "You dreamed, but what happened was also real."

Her mind must be functioning sluggishly. A dream was real? That seemed impossible. Yet the cat had been afraid of something.

"Tell me your dream," he said.

Gathering her wits, she began, doing her best to remember every detail. "Then the protective circle failed," she finished, "and there was nothing to stop—it—him—Shuck."

A muscle twitched in his jaw. "So you believed he'd been sent by someone to fetch you?"

Lucy nodded. "I don't know who. I remember wondering if the devil dog's master was as frightful as he is." A memory came to her. "Isn't it strange? In my dream of being a cat up in the magnolia with Persy, she warned me about Shuck without telling me what he was. I forgot about the name until just now." She grimaced. "I wish I could forget it permanently. It's a hideous name for a horrible beast."

"No one knows where the name originated," he said. "They've long known Shuck in the British Isles and also in France, where they call him something else. Shuck is old. He existed for centuries in Europe before the colonists brought him to America."

"You mean he's like a superstition, don't you?"

"If someone masters the art of summoning him, Shuck is real enough."

Lucy took another swallow of coffee before saying, "Now I understand what you meant about keeping an open mind, but I find this all so odd that I'm not sure I can." She clenched her mug. "I do know I don't ever want to dream about Shuck again."

Max sighed. "I'm afraid the next time won't be a dream. Dooley's persistent and dangerous."

"Joe?" She stared at him. "Are you saying Joe has something to do with that devil dog?"

Max leaned toward her. "Pay attention, Lucy. Use your head. Who else but Dooley would send Shuck to fetch you?"

"But I—but he—" She broke off, shaking her head. "It doesn't seem possible. I mean, Joe was—is—just this ordinary sort of guy."

"Nothing unusual ever?"

Lucy chewed on her lower lip before replying. "I did have a sort of hallucination when I met him, but that was me and not him, so it really doesn't count. I was looking in a window at an old movie poster of Dracula, when Joe came up behind me. He startled me and I sort of superimposed Dracula's face over his for an instant."

Max smiled grimly. "You're more skilled than you realize. Think. What do you have of Dooley's? I mean here, in this house."

"I don't have anything that belonged to him."

"Photos, surely."

"No. For some reason Joe was camera shy, though he did agree to wedding pictures. Which never got taken."

"Another thing to blame me for. Dooley must have given you gifts at some time or another, though."

"I didn't think of gifts as belonging to him. Yes, of course he gave me things. Flowers and candy, mostly."

"A romantic." Max's voice was strained, taut with some emotion she couldn't identify. "No keepsakes?" He glanced at the bare fingers of her left hand. "No engagement ring?"

"No, the wedding ring itself was set with diamonds and sapphires. But, of course, I don't have the wedding ring. His bridal gift—a necklace—was meant to go with the ring. I do have the necklace.'' She shook her head. ''I'm sorry I didn't think to take the necklace to the mansion and leave it there, because I certainly don't want it.''

''I'm sorry, too. That would have been a perfect solution, because returning the necklace to the place he last lived would be close enough to giving it back to him. You see, the gift is a link between you and Dooley. He's using it to reach you.''

''I wish I understood all this.''

Max rose. ''Where do you keep the necklace?''

''In my bedroom.'' She got up to show him and he trailed her into her room. She took the blue velvet box from the dresser and offered it to Max.

He refused to take it, saying, ''I'd rather not touch even the box.'' He frowned, staring at it. ''The shed,'' he said finally. ''The necklace has to remain with you until it's safe to return it to the mansion. The shed is at least some distance away from where you sleep, so that may help. But you must be the one to put the necklace there—no one else can.''

''Tonight?'' Her voice rose as she thought about going into the darkness and crossing the backyard where Shuck had been in her very real dream.

Max nodded. ''Now. With me.''

Actually, she'd wanted the necklace out of her house even before Max had insisted she hide it in the shed. If she couldn't accept all he'd told her, she did believe she was linked to Joe through the necklace, and she no longer wished to be. As for Shuck—how could a dream dog, no matter how horrible, harm her?

"All right," she said with some reluctance, still not completely convinced what she was doing was necessary.

She'd never before thought of the night as being unfriendly, especially when silvered by moonlight, but as they crossed the lawn toward the shed, only her pride kept her from clutching Max's arm and holding tightly to him. She started when Persy appeared from nowhere to dart ahead of them.

When they reached the shed, the night suddenly darkened. "A cloud crossing the moon," Max said matter-of-factly. "You'll have to go inside alone," he added. "I don't want to know exactly where the necklace is."

Persy had no such qualms and slipped into the shed ahead of her as soon as she opened the door. As quickly as she could in the darkness, Lucy knelt and eased the blue velvet box into a bushel basket full of empty plastic plant pots she'd been saving for no good reason. Satisfied she'd buried it deeply among the pots, she rose.

"Let's get out of here, Persy," she whispered to the cat.

As she stepped from the shed, the moon broke free of the cloud cover and something swooped over her head. Lucy stifled a scream, stumbling as she tried to duck. When Max's arms closed around her, she clung to him, burying her face against his bare chest and taking comfort in his warmth.

"Just an owl," he said soothingly. "I've seen him hunting at night before. You're safe."

With her head against his chest, she could hear the beat of his heart. At first slow and steady, as she listened the beat began to pick up speed. And then she realized her temporary fright had given way to another emotion entirely. It was no longer comfort she wanted from him.

He eased her slightly away to gaze down at her and she raised her face to look at him. "Safe?" she whispered.

"From everything except me," he murmured as his mouth slanted over hers.

His kiss asked no questions and offered no promises; she had no answers and she needed no promises. She was where she wanted to be and she gave herself up to the wonder of their embrace.

Not only their lips and bodies touched. Exciting as that was, in some way she didn't try to understand they also shared a bonding that had nothing to do with the physical.

Their kiss deepened and she savored his taste, a dark, mysterious flavor she couldn't get enough of. When he held her in his arms words like *belief* or *trust* were nothing but words; they didn't matter. He offered something beyond words, a blending of body and spirit she hadn't before realized was possible.

She ran her hands over his bare back, pressing closer, longing to be absorbed, to be a part of him. He cupped her against him so that she felt his need, a need that matched her own urgent yearning.

Why had she thought the night unfriendly? Honeysuckle-scented magic drifted on the breeze and enchantment rode the moon's silver light. Passion thrummed through her, rising from deep within, passion she'd never dreamed she possessed, a wild insistent passion roused by the man who held her, only by him.

"Tell me not to do this," he said hoarsely as he reached to untie the belt of her robe, opening it.

Instead of obeying, she shrugged off the robe, letting it drop at her feet. He groaned and put his mouth to her breast, his tongue hot through the gauzy cotton of her gown, hot and wet and indescribably thrilling.

He raised his head and looked into her eyes, his own shadowed by darkness. "Lucy," he whispered, "stop me."

She shook her head. She didn't want him to stop; she never wanted to stop; she wanted him to kiss and caress her forever. She wanted the night never to end, to last through eternity.

He lifted her off her feet and she wrapped her arms around his neck as he carried her across the lawn to the lounge. Still holding her, he eased down onto it, lying on his back with her on top of him. Taking advantage of her superior position, she put one hand to either side of his face and brushed her lips across his while tasting him with her tongue. A longing rose in her to taste every part of him.

Before she could begin, he lifted her hands from his face and took hold of her, rearranging her position so that her head was tucked under his chin. Holding her in place, he rasped, "You must know how much I want to make love with you. Ever since we met I've had one hell of a time trying to keep my hands off you.

The truth is I can't resist you. But it's also true that I must.''

"Why?" she whispered.

"Because of Dooley."

She stiffened. What did Joe have to do with this?

Max stroked her back, his hands lingering on the curve of her hips. "Why do you have to be so beautiful?" he asked. "How could any man resist you?"

If she relaxed, his caresses would carry her back to that wonderful place only Max could take her. But would it be the same now that he'd mentioned Joe's name? She knew it would not.

Pulling away, Lucy slid off the lounge. "You seem to be doing quite well at resisting me," she said tartly before stalking off to retrieve her robe. As she was tying the belt around her, she felt Max's hands on her shoulders. He turned her to face him.

"Damn it," he said, "Dooley's after you. How do you expect me to be able to keep him away if I'm so distracted by you that I can't think straight? An ordinary guy, you called him. He's no more ordinary than I am. Or than you are, for that matter. Why the hell do you think you attracted him in the first place? What do you think has me tied in knots every time I'm near you?"

Completely bewildered, Lucy shook her head. "I don't understand what you mean."

"You'd better start understanding if you mean to survive. Dracula?" He laughed, a short bitter laugh. "You were closer than you know."

More confused than ever, she said, "Vampires don't exist."

"We're not talking about movie vampires who sink their fangs in your neck and drain your blood, the fictional kind who can be thwarted by garlic or crosses. We're talking about what might be called a sixth sense, an extra sense that gives those who have it a kind of power the average man or woman doesn't possess. This power can be a blessing or a curse. It's a power that can be used for good or evil—the person who is born with it chooses. Or the power can be ignored and never used, difficult though that is."

"Are you saying that Joe is some kind of a—a vampire?"

"I'm saying he chose to use his power for evil."

"But you said—at least I think you did—that *I* have power. That's not true. I don't."

"Why do you think you saw through Dooley's facade to his rotten core?"

Lucy opened her mouth to protest, then hesitated, his words triggering the unwanted memory of being in St. John's Church and seeing the roses in her bridal bouquet rot away. And then Luke Cassidy's inexplicable change, a change only she detected...

"I—I used to have visions," she admitted unhappily. "They began when I was a child. But they went away. Until recently."

Max nodded. "Power."

She didn't want to have visions, didn't want him telling her she had power. But she was no longer a child who tried to shut out what she didn't wish to hear by covering her ears with her hands. She must face this and come to terms with what she was.

"You have this dreadful power, too?" she asked.

He lifted a hand from her shoulder to stroke her cheek. "Don't think of it as dreadful, Lucy. Really, it's not."

"I'm not convinced," she muttered.

He smiled wryly. "How can I think of it as dreadful, when the power I possess is the reason you're attracted to me?"

CHAPTER SIX

His arm around her shoulders, Max escorted Lucy to the door. "You'll be all right," he said. "Shuck won't be back tonight."

"You sent him away, didn't you?" she asked.

"Temporarily. On any permanent basis I can't control what Dooley does."

"Your power," she said hesitantly. "Is that how you knew I was in danger?"

He nodded. "We're attuned, you and I. We have been since that first kiss. Try to accept your own power and, if you can, learn to use it."

She sighed. "I'm not sure I want to."

"Maybe not, but if you're successful, you'll be less vulnerable to Dooley's attacks. To Shuck."

Feeling her involuntary shudder, he quelled the impulse to pull her closer to him. Her softness against him would be his undoing; he'd already used up his allotment of restraint. "Go inside," he said gruffly, "and lock the door. That's the only way I can guarantee you'll be safe for the rest of the night."

"But I thought you said Shuck wouldn't be back tonight."

"I mean safe from me," he told her.

She shrugged entirely free of him. "You make it sound as though I have no choice whatsoever. You said it was your power that attracted me. I don't know whether that's true or not. I'm not even certain I possess this power you claim I have.''

He started to speak, but she cut him off. ''I'm not finished.'' Determination and anger edged her words. ''Earlier you asked me to say no. That's one thing I *can* do. Don't worry about whether or not you're able to control yourself, because I've decided to grant your request. I've been told my grandmother used to insist that three times is a charm, so listen carefully—no, no and no.''

Without another word, she turned from him, opened the door and entered her house. He waited until he heard the click of the lock before starting back to Polly's. If Lucy believed in her grandmother's charm, she might be more potent than she realized— but he doubted if she did believe. He'd have to remember to ask her more about this grandmother of hers.

In the meantime he'd best shore up his own power. While he'd managed to rout Shuck, thus thwarting Dooley, he'd sure as hell screwed up otherwise. Lucy distracted him and distraction was dangerous.

This can't go on, he told himself. I've got to locate the bastard and get rid of him once and for all.

He'd never gotten as close to Dooley as he had in the church. Five years had passed since he'd stood over Olivia's grave and vowed to avenge her death. Because he'd inherited enough money to afford to be methodical, he'd first become a licensed private investigator so he'd have credentials, then taken on a few cases while he pursued his sister's killer. The cases made a good cover and his special ability was a help in quickly solving them. He didn't need the money.

For five years he'd been following her killer's trail, a trail littered with other victims. Since he knew what to look for, he'd become an expert in picking the killer's victims from media accounts of murders. Except for the last victim. This man had simply disappeared and Max, who'd been in Boston on a case of his own at the time, would never have connected him with his quarry if he'd been the kind who ignored seemingly trivial occurrences.

He was staying in a hotel. At breakfast in the coffee shop, he found, on the bench next to him, a *Globe* someone had been reading and left behind. The newspaper was open to an inner page and folded into quarters. Aware that nothing is truly random, before unfolding it to glance at the news, Max carefully checked every item on either side of the folds. The disappearance rated no more than one column, but that article was the only possible one he felt held any meaning for him.

Discreetly investigating, he found no clue to the man's whereabouts, but in seemingly casual conversations with people who'd known the missing man, Max learned enough to make him suspect Olivia's killer might be involved. If so, in all likelihood the missing man was dead—at least Max hoped he wasn't being kept semi-alive for Dooley's pleasure—and the body not yet discovered.

Once he'd cleared up his own case, Max pursued the matter by researching the background of the missing man and discovered a connection to a town in South Carolina. To Clover. Before going there, he'd learned what he could about the town and its inhabitants and the information convinced him that he was on a hot trail.

That was how, in St. John's Church, in Clover, he'd finally run the killer to earth. Unfortunately Dooley had recognized him and fled before Max could nail him. But this time Max had arrived before the next victim could be claimed. She was living bait to entice Dooley back to Clover so he could finish what he'd begun.

Never! Max vowed grimly. Lucy would *not* suffer Olivia's dreadful fate. Not while he was alive to prevent it.

He paused under the magnolia tree and scanned the night with his special sense, feeling Lucy's bright glow like a caress. There was nothing else to attract his attention, which meant Dooley was still too far away to be perceived, yet close enough to be able to send Shuck to fetch Lucy to him. Why in hell couldn't he get a fix on Dooley?

Persy brushed against his ankles and he bent to pick up the cat. "You've done enough guard duty for one night," he told the tabby. "We'll go in and try to grab some sleep."

Persy was the only one who did sleep. When the phone rang at seven the next morning, Max was already downstairs, fully dressed. Since Polly rarely came down before nine, Max took the call.

"Ryder? Maguire here. We may have a break—Dooley's license plate was spotted in Riverville. No one's doing anything about it. They're leaving it up to us. I just got the call."

"I'll check it out," Max said.

"Good, 'cause I won't be able to get away today."

After the sheriff gave him the details, Max hung up and hurried to his car. Riverville, he knew, was a small town to the north, set back a bit farther from the coast than Clover, and about a thirty-minute drive.

On the way, Max detoured past the Franklin mansion to make certain Dooley hadn't returned to hole up there. As he passed the closed iron gates, he recalled his trip inside those gates with Lucy.

A passing view of the tower thrusting above the pines started a muscle twitching in his jaw as once more he felt the wrenching conviction that Dooley had planned for Lucy's death to take place there. No doubt he intended to claim later that she'd fallen accidentally from one of the tower's long, narrow windows, because a fall from that height would go far to obliterate any telltale signs of how she'd really died.

Dooley hadn't been at the mansion when they were and he wasn't now, but there was something about the place that set Max's teeth on edge. He'd make damn sure Lucy never went near the Franklin estate again.

In Riverville, Max stopped and parked before reaching the Shady Acres Motel, where Maguire's informant had spotted Dooley's car. His special sense told him Dooley was not nearby, but caution led him to take a roundabout approach, coming into the motel grounds from the rear.

Max immediately spotted the car at the back of the property, parked in front of unit twenty-three, and paused to review the possibilities. Where was Dooley? Not in the car or in his room or anywhere close, so it was safe enough to look at the car.

When he did, he found the doors locked and saw a tan jacket lying on the passenger seat—nothing to show one way or another whether Dooley had abandoned the car there. When he turned away, he noticed a maid trundling her cleaning cart along the corridor. Taking a chance—he had no idea if Dooley had actually rented the unit or not—he called to her.

"Ma'am," he said, gesturing to the door of twenty-three, "I'm afraid I left my key in the room. Could you let me in to get it?"

She nodded. He held his breath as she inserted the master key in the lock. The door opened. He smiled and thanked her as he eased inside. A quick glance showed him no one was in the room at present, but it definitely was occupied by a man. Something troubled him, but he didn't have time to fix on it since he intended to exit immediately to conform to what he'd told the maid. No sense in arousing unnecessary suspicion.

Opening the door, he slipped a metal plate, made for the purpose, between the lock and the doorframe so the door couldn't automatically lock, left the room and closed the door behind him. Catching up to the maid, he handed her a couple of dollars and then sauntered toward the front of the motel.

As soon as she rounded a corner blocking Dooley's room from her view, Max wheeled and hurried back. After he entered he attached the Do Not Disturb sign to the outside of the door to avoid being interrupted. He felt the same warning prickle as before, but the source wasn't apparent.

Cautiously he looked over the room. The bed appeared slept in, dirty clothes were tossed on a chair, clean ones lay in an open suitcase and the bathroom had been in use. In a corner he spotted a blue floral carryon, unopened. Lucy's.

Dooley's room beyond a doubt. Not only had Lucy's carryon been in Dooley's car, obviously so had a suitcase of his own. Max had found Dooley's lair but not the beast himself. Nor could he pin down whatever it was that set his teeth on edge.

Now what? Max considered the options. Dooley must know they were searching for him and that his license plate was a dead giveaway. There was a good possibility this was a setup, intended to lure Max into waiting here in the hope of trapping Dooley when he returned. Lucy would then be left unguarded.

Damn! He should have thought of that before he left Clover. Dooley could be on his way there now. Max tamped down his rising alarm. If Dooley entered Clover during the day, he risked being recognized. Would he take that chance? Max clenched his jaw. He might.

Deciding Ford must be warned, he reached for the phone, only to discover it was inoperative. Dooley's work? Possibly not—it seemed illogical. Why would he bother, when there were countless other phones within easy reach once Max left the room?

He started for the door. Stopped. Staring at the corner where Lucy's carryon sat, he realized he was looking at the source of his uneasiness. What was wrong with the bag? Step by careful step he edged toward the floral patterned carryon. He halted within reach of the bag, appalled by the malevolent aura surrounding it. What had Dooley done and why?

An aberrant would sense the wrongness, but Lucy's power remained only partially developed, so she

might not—and a normal human definitely wouldn't.
A mental picture formed of Dooley paying someone
to drop the carryon off at Lucy's house. He saw her
bringing the bag inside and innocently opening it
without realizing her destruction might be waiting inside.

Was this Dooley's backup plan in case Max recognized he was being set up and didn't wait here for
Dooley to return? It very well might be. Whether it
was or not, Max didn't dare leave the carryon behind
for Dooley to use. But what the hell was he to do with
it?

Having no idea what malevolence lay within the
damn thing, he couldn't simply discard the carryon in
a Dumpster, lest some innocent person be harmed.
Fire would destroy any evil, but he could hardly set it
afire here. He might be able to decontaminate it with
the knowledge he possessed, but that would take time
and effort.

There was nothing he could do at the moment except see that the carryon wasn't left within Dooley's
reach. He wasn't foolish enough to grab the handles
with his bare hands—God only knows what might
happen to him if he did. Looking around for a way to
hold it, he spotted a fold-up umbrella leaning against
the wall near the bag. The crooked grip of the umbrella would be ideal.

Not until his hand was closing around the handle
did he sense any danger—and then it was too late. As
his fingers touched the umbrella, pain jagged through
him, paralyzing mind and body. He staggered away
from the carryon, cursing Dooley for his cleverness,
and fell helpless onto the bed. His last thought as the

malignant darkness sucked away his awareness was anger at how the bastard always managed to be one step ahead of him....

In the morning, Max's car was gone when Lucy left to go to work at the library. It wasn't there when she came home for lunch, or at four-thirty when she returned to the cottage. She was doing her best to keep her mind on what to fix for supper instead of wondering where Max was—with Mina?—when her brother phoned.

"I called Ryder at Polly's, but she says he's not there," Ford said. "Any chance you know where he is?"

"No, I haven't seen him all day and his car's gone," she replied. "Why?"

Ford hesitated so long she knew he was going to skirt the truth.

"I just wanted to talk to him. If you see him—"

"Have you checked with Mina Martin?" she inquired.

"What's she have to do with anything?" Ford asked.

Hating to admit she'd spoken before she'd thought, and determined not to reveal why, Lucy said, "Does this have something to do with Joe?"

"It might."

She drew in her breath, any consideration he might be with Mina forgotten. "Is Max in danger?" she demanded.

Ford chuckled. "Ryder in danger? From Joe Dooley? Come on, Sis, get real."

She realized her brother had no idea what had been going on. Max hadn't told him how dangerous Joe actually was.

"But if Max was supposed to call you, why hasn't he?" she asked.

"He wasn't supposed to. I thought he might, that's all. Since he hasn't, I figure he's probably doing a stakeout. Why are you so worried about the guy, anyway?"

"I wasn't until you phoned me," she snapped.

"Hey, you *are* upset. Want me to drop by?"

Lucy took two deep breaths, calming herself. "Thanks for the offer, but I'm okay. Really."

"You're sure?"

"Positive. You know I'd call you in a minute if I needed help." She made her tone as convincing as she could, not wanting her brother coming around and questioning her. She wasn't entirely sure how much she believed of what Max had told her and she didn't want to discuss anything he'd said or done with Ford.

Apparently she sounded convincing, because he said goodbye and hung up.

Stakeout, she mused. That meant Max had located Joe, or thought he had, and was waiting for him to return to wherever he was staying. Or to his car. Despite Ford's reassurance, she knew Max might well be in danger, and couldn't help worrying.

Unable to settle to anything, even fixing supper, she she finally dug in her closet and brought out the bridal underclothes she'd tossed inside, intending to busy herself with washing them so they could be donated to the hospital thrift shop.

Mixed up with the underwear she found her grandmother's moonstone necklace. How careless she'd been! "Sorry, Grandma," she said aloud, "but at least I didn't lose it permanently." Running it through her fingers, she admired the milky luster of the gems. Strange how the stones always felt warm to her touch.

Suddenly her fingers closed tightly around the necklace, as Max's face, contorted in pain, flashed before her. "Max!" she cried. "Max, what's wrong? Where are you?"

The vision vanished as quickly as it had appeared. Distressed, Lucy dropped the necklace on her bed and hurried from the room, intent on calling her brother and demanding to know exactly where Max was. Before she reached the phone, someone called her name. A man. Max? No, not his voice. Nor was it her brother's. She tensed. Had someone come into her house? She hadn't remembered to lock the front door after returning from work.

After a quick search through the cottage revealed she was alone, she paused at the front door to turn the key in the dead bolt. With her hand on the key, she paused, aware a picture was forming in her head, a picture of the Franklin mansion, the locked gates, the tower rising from the encroaching pines. Why was she visualizing this place she disliked?

The mental image grew more and more vivid, crowding every other thought from her mind. She must go there. Go to the estate. First, though, she had one other essential task to perform—she couldn't leave until it was done. There was no time to be wasted; she must hurry.

Lucy grabbed her purse from the chest near the door. As she was leaving the house, the vague feeling that she'd meant to call someone tugged at her, but she dismissed it, obsessed with the need to do what she must and then get in the car so she could reach the mansion as soon as possible....

Max struggled against the quicksand of darkness that sucked him down and down, threatening to consume him. He couldn't see or hear, he had no conception of time or place, nothing existed except the dark evil surrounding him. Though he couldn't measure how long he'd been in this malignant limbo, it seemed like forever. His continuing efforts to summon his power slowly grew more and more feeble. He had no idea where he was or how he'd gotten there, but he knew if he didn't escape soon he was doomed.

"Max!" a voice called. "Max, what's wrong?" A woman's voice. Her face flashed across the darkness and was gone, leaving only her cry of "Where are you?" behind to echo in his black hell.

With a tremendous thrust of his will, he remembered who she was. Lucy. Lucy Maguire. Other memories slipped into place. Dooley. Dooley had tricked him into this malevolent morass. Tricked him so that Lucy would be left unguarded. At Dooley's mercy.

"No!" he tried to shout. Could not.

As though his unspoken word had been a summons, he sensed he was no longer alone and that whatever had joined him in this place of horror was a new danger he must face. Hair rose on his nape as he fought to use his special sense to search the darkness.

And then Shuck materialized before him, lighted by a hellish red glow, mouth agape, his sharp teeth bloodred in the unnatural light....

As Lucy turned her car onto Highgate Road, she blinked and shook her head, suddenly realizing where she was. Where in heaven's name was she going? It couldn't possibly be to the Franklin estate—that was the last place in the world she wanted to go. And how had she gotten there? She didn't recall even getting into the car.

Feeling an unaccustomed heaviness around her neck, she raised her hand to find out why and touched the coolness of gemstones. She tilted the rearview mirror to look at herself, and in the fading daylight, she saw what she wore. Horror-stricken, she twisted the wheel so the car slewed onto the narrow shoulder. Stopping, she fumbled with the unfamiliar clasp of the sapphire-and-diamond necklace that had been her bridal gift from Joe.

How had it gotten around her neck? She would never willingly have placed it there. Nor did she recall retrieving the necklace from the shed. Terrified, she yanked it off, raised her hand to fling it out the window and suddenly held, trapped by a force she didn't understand, a force that made her forget what she'd meant to do with the necklace, forget that she'd intended to wheel the car around and drive home as fast as she could.

What am I doing parked here on the shoulder? she asked herself. I'm wasting time I can't afford. She gazed in confusion at the necklace in her hand, finally dropping it into her lap before gripping the wheel and pulling back onto Highgate Road, with the car still pointed toward the Franklin estate.

What was it she had to do at the mansion? Hadn't she already collected what she'd left there? Yes, she had, but not everything. Her blue silk suit and maybe her carryon were upstairs in one of the bedrooms and she had to get them—she couldn't delay.

Lucy shrugged off her uneasy feeling that her logic was somehow faulty and pressed her foot heavily onto the accelerator, making the little car shimmy and shake as the speedometer crept up and up past the speed limit. She had to hurry. It was important to retrieve her things and she'd rather be in and out of that place before night fell.

When she reached the iron gates, to her surprise they were open. The hair rose on her arms, but her compulsion to go on was greater than her sense of wrongness and she drove through the gates. She negotiated the winding road and reached the loop at the front of the house. Easing from the car, she stared at the huge house looming over her, all the windows dark, the pines crowding close as though to keep light away from the house altogether.

She'd never liked this place; at this moment she hated it and would give anything to be able to run back to her car and flee. But she could not. Swallowing her fear as best she could, Lucy climbed the steps, wondering if the front door would also be open and if she'd be able to bring herself to go in if so.

She found the door locked and breathed a bit easier as she searched through her purse for the key. Once she located it, she delayed, reluctant to insert the key and unlock the door.

"I don't want to be here," she whispered. "Why do I have to go inside?" The soft sound of her words seemed to echo abnormally loud in the beginning dusk, making her huddle in on herself.

Since you have to do what must be done, get it over with, she urged.

The entry hall lay in even deeper gloom than usual. She reached to switch on a light and hesitated. If she turned on a light, she would be announcing her presence, and she wasn't supposed to do that, although she didn't understand why no one must know.

Lucy shook her head in an effort to clear her mind, which seemed fuzzy. No, not so much fuzzy as divided, she decided—one part telling her she had no choice but to obey, the other part fearful, objecting to what must be done, even trying to fight against it.

She advanced into the entry, holding her breath as she made her way reluctantly through the shadows to the staircase leading to the second floor. Though she tried to believe the house was deserted, she somehow felt a presence hovered just beyond her comprehension.

At the top of the steps, Lucy saw the wide corridor was also gloomy, because all the bedroom doors were closed. Should they be? She couldn't remember.

Reaching the room where she'd left her blue suit, she opened the door. Pleased to find the bedroom perceptibly lighter than the corridor, she crossed the threshold, hurried to the closet and discovered her suit hanging exactly where it should be. Removing the suit, she glanced around for the carryon. The bag wasn't immediately visible, so she made a rapid tour of the room, stopping short when she reached the window.

Staring from the window into the gathering dusk, she caught back a frightened gasp.

When she'd arrived in her car, not a light showed in any window of the mansion, but now she saw a rectangle of light on the lawn. Somewhere in the house, a light had gone on, and from its location, she suspected it came from the room at the top of the tower, a place she'd never been. Lucy clutched the suit to her breast, feeling her heart thud in fearful apprehension.

Only one person would be in that tower.

Scarcely breathing, Lucy swung around to face the door. Gripping her purse as well as the suit, she tiptoed from the room into the corridor, intent on reaching the stairs as quietly and quickly as she could. She noticed a faint, unpleasant odor in the stale air, an odor that, although she couldn't identify it, she associated with evil. Goose bumps rose on her arms.

Instead of heading for the stairs, Lucy found herself turning toward the door to the tower. A bar of light slanting into the corridor showed her that door was ajar and she bit back a frightened whimper. The tower was the last place she wanted to go.

She struggled against continuing on toward the door—to no avail. Step by slow step, she advanced, even though she fought to retreat. The closer she came, the more foul the odor grew. But no matter how noisome, smells didn't turn on lights. People did. Joe. He was waiting for her in the room at the top of the tower stairs and he was forcing her to come to him.

Just as he'd forced her to put on his necklace and drive to the mansion. She hadn't been terrified then because she hadn't realized she had no free will or that he was influencing every one of her actions. Now she knew. Unfortunately, knowing didn't help her break the dreadful compulsion that made her push open the tower door and set her foot on the first step. The second. The third ...

CHAPTER SEVEN

Staring at the the devil dog poised to spring, Max knew that if Shuck reached him he would die. Hastily gathering what power he could, he made a desperate attempt to avert the monster's attack.

For a few moments it was touch and go, but as Shuck launched himself at Max's throat, he managed to erect a psychic barrier between himself and the beast. How long he could maintain the barrier was another matter. Whatever evil spell Dooley had woven into the umbrella continually drained Max's power, leaving him all but defenseless.

An eternity passed. With his entire attention fixed on funneling his diminishing power into protecting himself from Shuck, Max didn't at first notice when the black dog began to dissolve. When he finally realized Shuck was vanishing from his sight, exhausted relief overwhelmed all other emotion.

Eventually he regained enough curiosity to wonder what had caused Dooley, on the verge of winning, to release his hold on Shuck. When the probable reason filtered into Max's weary mind, a dark shroud of despair settled over him. Dooley must have temporarily set him aside to concentrate on Lucy, which meant she was almost within Dooley's grasp. Like Olivia, Lucy was doomed.

No! A violent surge of fury electrified Max, fueling his power. He fought furiously to free himself from the hellish labyrinth Dooley had thrust him into, desperately searching for a clue to the way back.

"Mister?" a woman's voice said. "You all right?"

Max fastened onto the voice, aware it was his salvation. Though he couldn't see anything but the darkness around him, he could hear her. Struggling to speak, he forced words, one at a time, from his paralyzed throat. "Help. Me."

Nothing happened and the voice spoke no more. An auditory hallucination? Max feared it had been. An eternity passed before he felt something—a hand?—touch his wrist. With the touch, Dooley's hold over him dissolved. Max's vision cleared. He stared up at the gray-haired man who'd touched him. Beyond the man hovered the maid Max had spoken to earlier. Had it been her voice he'd heard?

"Thanks," Max said hoarsely, endeavoring to push himself upright.

The man stepped back from the bed. "You'd best thank the Lord instead of me," he said. "I couldn't find no pulse, and I thought for sure you was a goner. The maids are supposed to check into all their rooms before they leave, even the ones with signs on the doors, so that's what Louisa did. She took one look at you and ran to the office crying and carrying on about the man in twenty-three dying, so I came to see. Mister, you sure did look like you was ready for the undertaker."

Hardly listening to this recounting of his rescue, Max swung his legs over the edge of the bed and sat without moving, waiting for his head to stop spinning. "I appreciate your help," he managed to say, "but I'm all right now."

"You still don't look so hot," the man said.

Max lurched to his feet, leaning against the wall. "Sorry to alarm you."

"Yeah, well, that's okay. You, uh, gonna be staying over?"

"Over?" Max repeated, belatedly realizing the man meant in the room. "No," he said, thinking as quickly as his sluggish mind permitted. "I won't be sleeping here, but I do need to leave some things in the room. I'll pay you for an extra night and come back to pick up my belongings tomorrow."

The man frowned. "Guess that won't be a problem."

"Good. Now, if you don't mind, I'd like to be alone."

Before closing the door behind himself and the maid, the man cast a last dubious look at Max.

Feeling as battered as if he'd gone twelve rounds with the current heavyweight champ, Max waited impatiently until his dizziness eased enough for him to check his watch. Appalled to note how late it was—he'd been out for hours—he started for the door, only to be brought up short by the sight of Lucy's carryon bag. He didn't dare leave such danger for anyone else to face.

Chafing at the delay, he found a wire hanger in the closet, twisted it into a hook, snagged the carryon's handles and gingerly lifted it. He eyed the umbrella and decided it was now harmless—he'd absorbed the evil. Holding the carryon carefully away from him, he left the room.

After reaching his car, he stowed the carryon in his trunk, still using the hanger as a handle. He got into the car, made a U-turn, tires squealing, then headed toward Clover. Toward Lucy. But would he be in time? Anguish twisted in his gut as he faced the possibility he might not be.

"Damn it, Lucy," he muttered. "Don't be his victim—reach for your power and fight. You can do it if you try. Fight!"

Lucy, now on the fifth step of the flight leading to the tower room in the Franklin mansion, halted, listening. Had she heard Max's voice? She could have sworn he'd spoken to her, one word: *fight.*

She glanced behind her, but he wasn't there. Had the voice been an illusion? No, she told herself, it was Max. When the moments passed, and he didn't appear, she realized with a sinking heart that what she'd heard had been within her own mind. While she acknowledged he might have spoken to her in this strange way, what good did it do? He wasn't here in the mansion, so how could he help her?

Fight? What did he think she'd been doing? She'd struggled against every step that brought her closer to the tower room. To Joe. She forced her thoughts away from what might happen to her once she reached the tower. If she gave in to terror she knew her fear would destroy the only weapon she possessed—the will to resist.

She'd long since grown immune to the nasty odor seeping from the tower, so it must be true what she'd read about smells—after lengthy exposure, the nose no longer reacts. Yet she could almost feel the noxious vapor swirling around her, adding to her revulsion and desperation.

Her right foot began to lift, seeking the sixth step. "No, you don't," she told her foot, using all her will to force it down again.

The compulsion to climb the stairs remained strong, but she'd discovered she could delay her climb by focusing on her feet. Though aware the delay might not be of any use, she kept at it, determined not to give in easily.

From the moment she'd met Joe, she'd become a doormat, letting him tell her what to do, what to wear, how to look, how to act. No longer. She wished she'd had the sense to stand up for herself from the beginning. If she had, perhaps Joe would have lost interest in her and none of this would have happened.

What did Joe want with her? No, she mustn't ask herself that question or her imagination might conjure up such horror she would be rendered totally helpless.

Despite her efforts, her right foot reached the sixth step and she struggled to keep her left where it was. If Max could send a mental message to her, why couldn't he come to her? Recalling her glimpse of his tortured face—another damned vision—she winced. Was he all right? She hoped the vision had been false. Her visions could as easily be illusions as truths, couldn't they? The bridal-bouquet vision had predicted truly enough, but how abut Luke Cassidy? That must have been an illusion, pure and simple.

Perceiving all her efforts had been in vain—she now stood completely on the sixth step—for a moment her resolve to remain brave faltered. She stiffened her spine. She might be terrified, but she refused to snivel and whimper or stop trying. Her brother had always praised her courage. Max also must be convinced she could fight or he wouldn't have told her to. They believed in her; she would believe in herself and *not* give up.

Vampire. What use would courage be against such a creature? Lucy swallowed convulsively. Her vampire vision of Joe surely had been illusion. Except Max had insisted she'd seen true. Joe might not be a vampire in the Dracula mold, but he was equally dangerous, Max had said. Dangerous how?

What waited for her at the top of the stairs?

"Lucy." The sinister murmur slithered down from the tower and into her ears. "Lucy. Come to me, my eager bride."

His words coiled in her mind, as poisonous as the water moccasins that glided through the Carolina swamps, and sent the venom of terror spurting through her. A shudder rippled through Lucy. The voice might sound like Joe's, but whoever—whatever—spoke to her from the tower wasn't the man she'd thought she knew, the man she'd come far too close to marrying. Joe, yes, but yet not Joe. Deadly danger crouched at the top of the stairs she was trying so hard not to climb.

"Come, Lucy," he ordered, his voice smooth and sweet as honey. "It's impossible to resist—you know you belong to me."

Her mind blanked by fear, she didn't realize she'd moved until she found herself on the next step, the seventh. Her foot was lifted to climb, when suddenly something grabbed her from behind, pulling her off balance. A picture of Shuck's vicious fangs flashed before her and she opened her mouth to scream.

A hand cut off the scream before it emerged. Numb with fright, she felt herself being dragged down the steps, down to the second-floor corridor, where she was scooped into a man's arms, head flopping against his chest as he raced toward the staircase to the ground floor.

Too dazed to think clearly, Lucy didn't understand what was happening until Max's characteristic scent seeped into her awareness. With a moan of relief, she buried her face against him, clinging to him with such tenacity that he had difficulty detaching her when they reached his car.

"Let's go!" he ordered after thrusting her into the passenger seat.

She forced herself to loosen her grip, and seconds later he swung behind the wheel and the car shot along the winding drive. She didn't take a deep breath until they were through the gates and barreling along Highgate Road. Speech was still beyond her.

"Close call," Max said.

Lucy made three attempts before any words came out and the ones that did surprised her. "I was on the seventh step."

Max shot her a glance. "Of how many?"

"Twenty-one. He said so once. I didn't want to go up to the tower, but I couldn't—" her voice broke "—stop myself. He—" To her dismay she burst into tears.

"I know." Max's voice was grim.

She longed to collapse against him, to seek comfort in his solid warmth, but held herself away. Irrational though the notion might be, she felt it was unsafe to touch Max right now. He mustn't be distracted in any way. This strange thought stopped her flow of tears. She unearthed a crumpled tissue in a pocket of her jeans and dabbed at her wet face.

"What the hell were you doing at the mansion, anyway?" Max suddenly demanded.

His question triggered an onslaught of confused images—the shadowy mansion, seeing the light from the tower, the blue suit, the diamond-and-sapphire necklace . . .

Her hand flew to her throat, feeling for a weight that was no longer present. "The necklace he gave me," she cried. "Where is the necklace?"

"No longer hidden in the shed, I take it."

"I was in my car," she said slowly, reaching for an elusive memory, "and I remember I took off the necklace. But I don't know what I did with it."

"I retrieved your purse from the upstairs hall," Max said. "No necklace inside."

A new thought stabbed through her, making her ignore the fact that he'd searched her purse. "My car! I left my car at the mansion."

"Ford and I will collect the car tomorrow. I have something I want to leave there, anyway. So you went to the mansion to get your blue suit?"

Lucy frowned. "Not exactly. I mean that was in my mind, yes, but—" She shook her head. "Somehow I *had* to go, as if it wasn't really my choice."

"Once you put the necklace on, he'd have no trouble compelling you to come to him."

Blinking back another threat of tears, she hugged herself and said, "I must have taken the necklace from the shed, but I don't remember at all."

"I wish I knew where the damn thing was. If he finds the necklace—"

Max paused and didn't go on, leaving Lucy more upset than ever. Trapped in the frightening labyrinth of her thoughts, she said nothing, and he didn't speak again.

Even after she was inside her cottage, watching Max lock the dead bolt, her fears remained. "I don't feel safe even now," she admitted.

"Wise," Max said tersely. "Because you're not."

Lucy didn't want to be told she was right—she wanted reassurance. "Don't leave me," she pleaded, ashamed to be asking, but unable to help herself.

"I don't plan to. It's too late to nab the bastard anyway, even if I were in any shape to try. He'll be long gone from the Franklin estate. Gone with what's left of Joseph R. Dooley, leaving nothing behind but the stink."

She stared at him in total confusion.

"I need something to eat," Max said, "and we both could use a couple jolts of coffee before I try to explain."

Once in the kitchen, she regained her equilibrium. No matter what horror she'd left behind, busying herself with familiar tasks like making coffee and re-warming a leftover beef-and-noodle casserole steadied her nerves.

He polished off the remainder of the casserole and settled back with his third cup of coffee before saying a word. "Thanks. You're not a bad cook."

"You downed my cooking so fast I'm amazed you could even taste it," she told him. "You ate as though you were starved."

"I was. Any dessert?"

Lucy started to offer him a piece of what was left of her peach cobbler, then shook her head and put the cobbler pan itself on the table with a clean fork.

He gave her a lopsided grin. "You catch on fast. I like that in a woman."

Again he finished what was left. She put the pan in the sink to soak along with the casserole dish, then rejoined him at the table. While he was eating, she'd made up her mind she had to know the worst.

Looking him in the eye, she said, "You called Joe a kind of vampire. I want to know what would have happened to me if you hadn't arrived in time."

He gave her a long, level look before nodding. "What I say will be the truth. Whether you can accept it or not is up to you. First of all, understand that what he tried to do may have failed because he was hampered by being in a hurry. He knew there was a possibility I might escape his traps. Or be able to free myself if I did fall into one—which I did. He must have been in real need of renewing his energy or chances are I might not have escaped."

Lucy gazed at him with surprise, having difficulty imagining Max being bested in any circumstances. But it did explain her vision of him. "Joe trapped you? No wonder you were in agony."

"So you *did* see me. I wasn't sure." Max was pleased.

She put his words aside to be examined later, when she knew more. "Never mind that now. You haven't answered my question."

"The man you call Joe is a psychic vampire." Max's voice showed no emotion. "If he'd succeeded in luring you to the tower, first he would have raped you, because your pain and fear would have given him an extra fillip as he drained your power along with your life force. You'd have been dead when he finished.''

Horror rendered her speechless. Incredible as the explanation was, she felt the truth of it deep within her bones.

Max reached across the table and touched her hand. ''I won't let him have you, Lucy. Never.''

How could he, how could anyone, stop a vampire? She rose abruptly, wanting to flee, with no place to run to. She was safe nowhere.

Max got to his feet and led her into the living room, where he pulled her down next to him on the couch and put his arm around her. She sat stiffly for a moment or two before giving way to her desperate need for comfort.

Burrowing her face in his chest, she snuggled as close to him as she could get.

''He failed,'' Max said softly. ''Remember that. We outwitted him.''

The truth of what he said gradually filtered through to Lucy, finally enabling her to stop clinging so frantically to Max. She eased away until she was merely resting against him. They sat in silence for a time until she remembered her message.

''My brother wants you to call him,'' she said.

''Later. I've nothing to tell him except that Dooley got away. Again.''

''You could try telling him what you've just told me. The truth.''

Max shook his head. ''He couldn't accept it. And if by some odd chance he did he'd be at risk because he'd try to handle things his way. He might well be killed, since I'm far from certain I could protect him. The man I'm after is more dangerous than your brother can possibly imagine.''

After thinking over what he'd said, Lucy sighed. Max was right; Ford would never understand. How could he, when she wasn't sure she did, even though she could find no other explanation for what she'd been through.

Max stirred, shifting position until he gazed down at her. "I never thought I'd hear myself saying this while holding you in my arms, but I have to admit I need sleep. We both do. And since I'm not leaving you alone, that means I'm staying here.''

In his eyes Lucy saw the question he didn't ask. She had no intention of telling him to use the couch; after what had happened to her at the mansion, she needed Max within reach. "I'm too scared to sleep alone,'' she admitted.

He gave her a twisted grin. " 'Sleep' being the key word. Fair enough. I'm a perfect gentleman while asleep.''

"Is it safe? To sleep, I mean.''

His smile faded and he nodded abruptly. "I'll set wards that should protect us for a while.''

She found her tension easing and realized she'd come to trust this man, no longer a stranger, who'd thrust himself into her life. If Max said she could sleep in peace, she knew she would.

Lucy left him in the living room, muttering unintelligibly as presumably he set wards, and entered the bedroom. Seeing her grandmother's moonstone necklace coiled on the bed, she shook her head, not recalling that she'd placed it there. How confused she must have been when she'd left the house earlier. After laying the moonstones on the dresser, she decided her nightgown was too revealing to wear and took a long T-shirt with her into the bathroom.

By the time she was ready to crawl into bed, Max, still in his jeans, lay deeply asleep on top of the covers. She threw a quilt over him, then stood gazing down at him, thinking that even in sleep his face seemed guarded. Yielding to impulse, she gently caressed his stubbled cheek with her fingertips before easing onto the other side of the double bed.

Exhaustion, combined with the solid comfort of Max's body next to her, allowed her to slide quickly into sleep's dark tunnel.

The next she knew, her grandmother stood at the foot of the four-poster bed. "I bequeathed you my power," Grandma said with some asperity. "Why do you turn away from knowledge, why must you wear blinders to avoid seeing?"

Lucy stared at her grandmother, unsure whether she was dreaming or actually confronting an apparition. Grandma looked so real, exactly as she had in the photograph, with her shrewd blue eyes that penetrated inside a person. Again Lucy could smell the rose scent that seemed to cling to the moonstone necklace, a scent she associated with Grandma Maguire.

Her hair is cut like mine, Lucy realized in amazement. Except for the gray streaks, it's exactly the same color. Did I unknowingly imitate Grandma? she wondered.

As if she'd asked the question aloud, her grandmother replied, "Of course you're like me, child, like me in every way. You always have been. Why do you refuse to use what you've been gifted with?''

"I have no special gift," Lucy protested.

"Nonsense. What you mean is you keep rejecting that gift. Such foolishness has led you deeper and deeper into danger. Look into yourself and learn before it's too late." Grandma's gaze shifted from Lucy to the sleeping Max. "Do you want him to die?"

"No!" The denial burst from Lucy as she understood how bleak her life would be without Max.

"Then take heed before it's too late."

"What is my gift?" Lucy cried. "How can I learn to use it?"

"You and you alone must discover that for yourself. And you'd best hurry." As she said the last word, Grandma vanished as suddenly she'd appeared.

Lucy took a deep breath. A dream, she tried to tell herself, uncertain whether she was asleep or awake, or whether she was thinking the words or muttering them. I'm having a dream.

"No dream." Max's voice startled her. "Your grandmother was here in this room."

Had he really spoken? Now certain she was awake, Lucy sat up and stared at him, but it was too dark in the bedroom to see his face. "Max?" she whispered.

He didn't answer. Listening, she heard his heavy, rhythmical breathing. Either he truly was asleep or pretending to be. She touched his shoulder. "Max?"

He sat up abruptly, his hand clamping down on her wrist. "What?" he demanded harshly. "What's wrong?"

"N-nothing," she stammered, taken aback. "I thought you spoke to me."

He released her wrist and leaned back against the headboard. "What did you think I said?"

"You told me my grandmother was here."

"Maybe she was."

"Then you did speak to me?"

"Not out loud, but that doesn't mean you didn't hear me in a different way—you have the ability to."

Lucy propped a pillow against the headboard and leaned back, too. "That's what she told me. My grandmother, I mean. That I have some kind of gift. But it had to be a dream."

"Why?"

Lucy found she couldn't answer. She'd been forced to accept the reality of a terrible, unreal creature like Shuck, so why couldn't her grandmother's ghost visit her?

Though a vision of Grandma Maguire was far less frightening than the devil dog, what had happened when she was nine made Lucy apprehensive. Had she really seen her grandmother on that awful night? Had Grandma's ghost actually spoken to her then?

Lucy remembered her ninth birthday party, where her father had presented her with the moonstone necklace. Fascinated by the shifting opalescence of the milky stones, she'd kept the necklace on the stand next to her bed. The terror began that same night.

Roused by a voice she didn't recognize, Lucy had opened her eyes to see an older woman with curly gray-streaked dark hair bending over her.

"Look, child," the woman had said before vanishing. "Take heed when the moonstones glow."

On the bedside stand, the stones gleamed in the dark like warning beacons. Then came Lucy's first vision, one so horrible she thrust it away from her, unable to bear what she saw. Clutching the necklace, she leaped from her bed and ran to her parents' room for comfort. Finding their bedroom empty, she began to wail.

When her big brother, Ford, stumbled into the room, demanding to know what was wrong, Lucy clung to him, sobbing out an incoherent story of terror and death. All he took in was the realization it was almost morning and their mother and father were not in the house.

Later, after Ford searched for them and eventually discovered them dead, along with the man involved in their tragic love triangle, he withheld the truth from Lucy, telling her she'd had a nightmare.

Lucy longed to believe it had been no more than a nightmare, even when she learned the terrible truth and understood it was what she'd seen in her vision. Because she didn't want to accept this, she had closed her mind, refusing to believe in visions. Since she associated the moonstone necklace with her parents' death, she had hid it, never opening the jewel case.

Damn Max for forcing her to remember what she'd kept buried all these years.

Turning on him, she accused, "My world's turned upside down since you appeared. I don't know what to believe anymore."

"Believe in me," he said softly.

She turned toward him, seeing only the outline of his face in the darkness but aware he was looking at her.

He stroked her cheek with his fingers. "As you touched me earlier," he murmured.

"You were asleep!" she blurted.

"I always know when you're near me and your touch reaches through to me even when I sleep."

His words and his touch warmed the chill that had settled inside her while she was in the mansion, a chill that had remained until this moment. When his hand left her face, she involuntarily leaned toward him, not wanting to lose the contact.

"Lucy," he murmured, "bright and shining Lucy. Much as I want you, I can't risk any more linkage than we already share. If we make love, chances are the bond will prove unbreakable and that scares me."

She pulled back. Was she willing to risk what he described? "Do you mean Joe could use the bond against us?" she asked.

"My reasons have nothing to do with him." His tone warned her off.

"Why did you call me 'bright and shining'?" she asked after a moment.

"Because your power shines through, brightening your aura, until you gleam like the evening star."

She sighed in frustration. "What is this power you and Grandma claim I have? In my dream—or whatever it was—she urged me to use it, but she wouldn't or couldn't tell me how. Will you?"

"You know you have the ability to see ahead, plus the gift of seeing the truth within people."

She still couldn't be sure her visions were what he claimed: a look into the future or a glimpse behind a facade. But the evidence of the past added to what she'd seen the last few months was incontestable. "I did see *you* earlier today," she admitted, speaking as much to herself as to him.

" 'In agony,' I believe you put it. I was." His voice was devoid of emotion.

"You mentioned traps. What happened?"

"I wasn't as careful as I should have been."

Again the finality in his words told her he didn't mean to discuss it further.

"Even if I accept my visions as fact," she said after a moment, "I still don't understand what brings them on. Or how to control them."

"Since your grandmother appeared to you, they must be connected to her in some way."

His hand closed over hers, his clasp warm and reassuring.

"Don't struggle to make a connection. Just let your mind drift until the answer comes to you unsought."

Is that what Grandma Maguire's ghost meant when she said she'd bequeathed me her power? Lucy asked herself. Did I inherit this unwanted gift from her? Shaken by this possibility, Lucy tried to obey Max's suggestion about letting her mind drift, closing her eyes and leaning back against the pillow that she'd propped against the headboard. Bright yellow and green swirled behind her closed lids in a chaos of color, forming patterns she tried to decipher—with no success. Recalling his insistence on not struggling, she tried to disengage her consciousness and simply observe the swirling brightness.

When she felt herself drifting she didn't fight, and soon her only link to her room and her bed was the warmth and solidity of Max's hand. The colors muted, becoming a circular glow that dispersed into seven smaller circles and began to form a ring that she knew would be her answer. But before the ring was complete, a blot of darkness marred the image, expanding until it extinguished the glow.

Sensing danger, Lucy fought to bring herself back to the bed where she lay with Max, their fingers entwined. Before she could, the darkness formed an image of its own, a frightening image with sinister red eyes and a gaping mouth full of sharp teeth.

"Shuck!" she screamed.

CHAPTER EIGHT

Even as Lucy's scream jolted through Max, he felt her hand go limp in his grasp. He tightened his grip, knowing that his only chance of reaching her was through this physical link. If he couldn't find her, he had no chance to save her. He hadn't anticipated Shuck's attack—once again he'd made the mistake of underestimating his opponent.

He drew the unconscious Lucy into his arms, sliding her shirt up with his free hand for more skin contact between them. The closer together they were, the better his chance of intervening and thwarting the attack.

Not allowing himself to be distracted by the soft crush of her breasts against his chest, Max gathered his energy for the search and then left his body and plunged into Shuck's hellish red-lighted darkness. Almost immediately he sensed the presence of Lucy's spirit, but when he tried to home in on her tiny glow, psychic barriers blocked his way to her. Shuck had been programmed to expect him.

No matter what maneuver he tried, Max couldn't find a way past the barriers. If Shuck wasn't stopped, the devil dog would deliver Lucy's spirit to the man who called himself Dooley. With her spirit held hostage by Dooley, her body would die within a matter of hours.

He means to make me come to him to bargain for Lucy's life, Max told himself. And he has no intention of keeping any bargain he might make. He wants not only Lucy, but me, as well.

He'll get neither of us.

Summoning all the energy he had left, Max focused on Lucy's glow, doing his best to contact her in the hope that she'd receive his sending and know he was near. If he could reach her in this way, the barriers wouldn't matter. Time after time he tried, but she made no response. He was about ready to give up the effort, when he finally made contact—but not with Lucy. An image rose before him. He had no idea who was responsible for the sending, but there it was, the image of a moonstone.

The moonstone's muted light offered a beacon of promise in the sinister red haze. Without being told, he understood that Lucy must be made to see the moonstone image as clearly as he did, though he didn't know why. He shifted his energy to the image, meaning to test it against the barriers. Would the image pass?

Instead of moving toward the barriers, like the moon it was named for the image of the gem arced up and up, rising high above. Rays of soft, pale light penetrated the red gloom, bypassing the barriers and mingling with Lucy's tiny glow.

Only gradually did Lucy become aware of a change. Shuck's fangs still menaced her, but she noticed he now was bathed in an opalescent light that seemed to be slowly soaking up his darkness. The light reminded her of her grandmother's moonstones. Of the necklace that had been passed on to her. The necklace meant for her to use. The moonstone necklace.

An image of the necklace came to her, of the seven stones set at intervals along the heavy gold chain. As she pictured it, the rays from above strengthened, beaming through the crimson haze, surrounding Shuck and blotting him out with their pearly light.

At the same time, she felt a tug at her hand, though no one was with her. She sensed no peril in the contact and so, lost in the shimmering haze, not knowing her way back, she let herself be led by the tugging. Without a way to measure time, Lucy had no notion of how long she traveled before she saw Max coming toward her. And yet—was it Max?

How could he appear so tenuous, as though made of mist?

Hurry, he urged, without speaking. Though confused, she obeyed. When she came within reach, his right hand, almost transparent, grasped her left. The next she knew she lay in her bed, in Max's arms, and he was as solid as ever.

"We're safe for the moment," he assured her.

Lucy freed her hand from his so she could cling to him; he was the only constant in a world that seemed to have shifted alarmingly from familiar to alien.

"It wasn't a nightmare?" she asked, fearing she already knew the answer.

"You had a first time out-of-body experience," he told her. "My fault the trip turned out to be so frightening. I should never have urged you to let go. I knew my wards couldn't protect you once you left your body—my only excuse is that I didn't foresee you'd wind up doing just that."

They lay so close she could feel his warm breath against her cheek as he spoke. With her bared breasts cushioned against the springy hair of his chest, that wasn't all she felt. A warmth that had nothing to do with comfort diffused through her, leaving her breathless.

She didn't want to dwell on danger; she was in no hurry to listen to explanations. All she wished for at the moment was to be held close to Max and feel the sweet languor of need pulse through her.

"Lucy," he said.

Thrilled to hear the rasp of desire in his voice, she snuggled closer.

"Lucy," he repeated. "We can't—"

"Yes, we can," she murmured, shifting in his arms so she could kiss him.

He groaned when her lips met his, crushing her against him as he deepened the kiss. He tasted of secret, wonderful darkness, but there was nothing mysterious about his obvious desire. He wanted her. The conviction came to her that she must do everything within her power to urge him into making love with her. Now. More was involved than their mutual passion, this was the right time, whether he realized it or not. He mustn't draw back.

Giving herself up to the hot sweetness thrumming through her, she pressed against him, her hands caressing his face, his shoulders, his back, her fingers sliding down under the waistband of his jeans, her need fueled by his increasing excitement.

"Lucy, Lucy," he whispered, his lips against her throat. "How tempting you are."

She sensed this was his moment of decision. What more could she do to tip the scales in the way they must go? With one quick movement, she eased back, pulled her rucked-up T-shirt over her head and flung it away. Letting her desire guide her, she traced his lips with the tip of her tongue, then trailed down along his throat to his chest and then lower, alternately licking and nipping his skin.

When she reached the barrier of his jeans, she slowly retraced her path, savoring his taste and his scent, as her need for him spiraled higher and higher.

His hands found her breasts, then he caressed them with his lips and tongue until she moaned in unrestrained pleasure. He hooked a finger under the top of her bikinis, pulled them down and off, flipped onto his back and slid her on top of him, cupping her buttocks to press her against his jean-covered arousal.

She sat up, straddling him, opened the snap holding his jeans closed and pulled down the zipper. In a sudden, swift movement, he tipped her from him so she lay on her back and then he yanked off his jeans. Her legs parted involuntarily as he eased between her thighs, where his caresses made her cry out in pleasure.

At last he rose over her and slowly, sweetly, slipped inside her. She caught her breath at the never-before-felt sensation of delicious invasion. Hearing his breath rasp in his throat, she realized vaguely he must be having difficulty keeping himself under control, but she lost the thought as his gentle thrusting set her afire.

She wriggled her hips, urging him on, needing more and more and more, until at last he groaned and plunged fully inside her. No longer aware of her surroundings, she gave herself up to the magic they'd created between them, traveling with him beyond imagination.

When reason returned, she found herself cuddled in his arms.

"You seduced me," he murmured. "I'll admit I enjoyed the experience immensely, but virgins aren't supposed to know how."

"I had to," she told him. "It was time."

"Time," he repeated. "How do you know?"

"I felt it."

He traced her lips with his finger. "You don't understand what you've brought about, do you?"

She sighed in remembered pleasure. "I'm totally aware we made love."

"Our lovemaking bonded us—irrevocably. Do you realize what that means?" Without waiting for a response, he answered the question he'd posed. "Only death can release either of us from that bond, Lucy."

She wondered why he seemed so upset. "Till death do us part?" she said. "That's in the marriage ceremony, but we're certainly not married."

"And I never *do* intend to marry."

His words and the grim tone of his voice cast a shadow on the glow of her happiness. Did he think she had expected him to ask her? "I certainly have no plans to propose to you," she said tartly, edging away from him. "Or to any other man. Once bitten, twice shy, as my mother used to say."

"Marriage has nothing to do with the damn bond," he said gruffly, pulling her back into his arms. "We're aberrants, as I've told you before, and we're different in more than one way from most humans. We've been drawn to each other from the moment we came face-to-face, which is common with people like us. So common that I thought I could handle it. I was wrong. The attraction didn't remain at merely warm feelings, but heated up so quickly there was no chance for either of us to escape its wildfire. In case you haven't noticed, I'm still burning.''

His mouth covered hers in a kiss that showed her exactly what he meant, igniting her own blaze. Nothing mattered but Max and the passion flaring between them. . . .

Once bitten, twice shy be damned, Max thought, telling himself Lucy's mother could well have pointed out that one might as well be hanged for a sheep as for a lamb. It was already too late for him to avoid the inevitable bonding, so why not make love with Lucy again? And again and again. God knows he'd wanted to from the moment her brother had brought them together.

So making love with her was dangerous and could lead nowhere. Little difference that made when she lay naked in his arms.

The thrill of being the first man to taste her exquisite sweetness still echoed in his mind as well as his body. She'd become truly his at that moment. He didn't think she realized that, at the same time, he'd become hers, whether he'd wanted to be or not. Bonding between aberrants wasn't always by choice and when it happened the bond became permanent.

As he tasted the honeyed lure of her mouth, he felt a purely masculine impulse to shout a challenge to Dooley, to inform the bastard that she was his and his alone and that he'd fight to the death rather than allow Dooley to come anywhere near her.

Buoyed by the euphoria brought on by making love with her, he was convinced he could best not only Dooley but any man who tried to come between Lucy and him. Could and would.

How soft her skin was, how exciting her scent. Words weren't adequate to tell her how lovely she was and how much he wanted her, so he tried to show her by the intensity of his passion. Her eager response to each caress assured him that her desire matched his own, making the flames burn hotter and hotter. When he felt her open to him, body and spirit, offering all of herself, he lost the ability to think, to reason. Nothing existed except Lucy and the sensuous magic of their joining.

Though he hadn't fully trusted any one since his sister's death, caught by the strength of the bond he shared with Lucy, he found himself helpless to do anything but offer himself to her in the same, open, vulnerable way that she'd given herself to him.

When he finally descended from the heights to the mundane, Max fell asleep, still holding Lucy. He awoke to daylight sneaking around the edges of the curtains at her bedroom windows, awoke to daylight and to brooding over what had happened between them.

Glancing at the sleeping Lucy next to him, he sighed, wondering how he could possibly wrestle his mind back on track when she lay within his reach. Forcing himself to turn away from her, he eased from the bed, retrieved his discarded clothes and headed for the bathroom.

A quick shower later, he stood at the open back door, gazing into a foggy morning. When Persy ambled over, Max opened the screen door and picked up the cat, cuddling her in the crook of one arm while he petted her.

"Nothing like a good watchcat," he told her, "and you're one of the best. It wasn't your fault we almost lost Lucy last night. I take full blame."

Persy's response was to close her eyes and purr.

"I have to nail the bastard before he tries again," Max went on, "but how?"

The cat blinked and began licking Max's fingers. When he started to take his hand away, she nipped it, not breaking the skin but hard enough to be uncomfortable. Then she leaped from his arms, marched to the refrigerator and sat down.

"Talk about biting the hand that feeds you," he muttered as he followed her. He was dumping tuna into a dish for Persy, before he made a connection between his question and her nip. Had she answered him in her feline fashion?

It made no sense at first, but when he turned the idea around—feed the hand that bites you—he saw a possibility. Dooley had to be hungry, his energy level lowered by the effort to trap Lucy and to kill Max Ryder. Offer Dooley a chance to feed. Dangle an irresistible lure to entice him from hiding and then spring the trap.

Max grimaced, aware of the problem of setting up a trap Dooley wouldn't sense. At the same time, he had a fair idea of how to go about it. After he constructed and set the trap, though, who was he to use for the lure? Whoever he chose would be at risk, no matter how carefully he tried to protect her. Definitely not Lucy; she was already in too much peril.

Even as he wondered if he had the right to endanger an innocent person, Mina Martin popped into his mind. When she'd come on to him that day in the diner she'd hinted, none too subtly, that she was eager to glimpse the interior of the Franklin mansion. What if he asked her instead of Ford to help him retrieve Lucy's car?

Dooley, he was positive, would be holed up somewhere close to the estate, perhaps even somewhere on the grounds. Mina was no aberrant, but her lively vitality should be attractive to Dooley, especially in his deprived state.

The problem was how to keep Mina from being harmed while she enticed Dooley into the trap. Max didn't like the idea of leading her unwarned into danger, but there was no use trying to explain to her. She would think him mad.

Would wards be sufficient protection for Mina? Maybe. Dooley might be powerful, but he was weakened by his lack of psychic nourishment. His efforts to lure Lucy to him took copious energy and he couldn't go after another aberrant, one with the shining energy he really craved, until he feasted off his chosen victim—Lucy.

But he could attack ordinary humans. While continuing to stalk Lucy, Dooley could, and probably was, using such energy as he could glean from the people around him. So far, possibly because he wanted to keep a low profile, he didn't seem to have left any of his victims dead, which meant he was taking barely enough energy to sustain himself.

Max wasn't happy with his plan to place Mina at risk to trap Dooley, but the bastard must be stopped before Lucy came to any harm, and Max could think of no other way.

Leaving Persy in the house, he scribbled a note to Lucy, picked up a set of extra keys, locked her back door behind him and strode toward his room at Polly Smith's, not liking to abandon Lucy but aware that his bond with her would warn him if anything threatened her.

When he reached Polly's he was still mulling things over. With his hand on the phone, he finally decided to leave it up to fate and punched in the number of the sheriff's office.

Moments later he hung up. Ford was out of town, so he obviously couldn't go with him to the Franklin estate to retrieve Lucy's car. Fate seemed to have given him Mina, instead. He regretted having to use her and vowed to do all his power allowed to protect her. Her risk and his should be minimal. He realized, though, that he was willing to hazard anything to protect Lucy.

Max set to work on the trap immediately. Once it was ready for him to put in place, he'd call Mina. Intent as he was on protecting Lucy, still he almost hoped Mina would refuse to go out with him.

Lucy, disappointed to find Max gone when she awoke, read the note he'd left in the kitchen. "He says he has some work to do," she complained to Persy, "and that he'll be back before dark. Okay, I can live with that. I'm going to work myself. But couldn't he have given a slight hint of how he feels?"

Persy, busily washing herself, made no comment.

The phone rang. Lucy jumped up to answer it then hesitated, fearing the call might be from Joe. On the other hand, it could be Max. She lifted the phone.

"Lucy?" Katie's voice sounded tentative.

Lucy immediately felt guilty. "I've been meaning to call you," she said. Which was the truth. Katie was her best friend.

"Are you okay?"

"More or less," Lucy told her.

"Could we get together for lunch?" Katie asked.

"Sounds great. Come by the library around noon?"

After Katie agreed and hung up, Lucy realized with a pang just how negligent she'd been. Ordinarily she and Katie saw each other at least once a week and told each other everything. Now, though, she had things she wasn't ready to share with her friend. Come to think of it, maybe Katie did, too. For example, though Lucy knew very well Katie had been in love with Luke Cassidy when he left Clover, Katie hadn't mentioned Luke's name once since his return with his young son.

Slow days at the library often dragged and today was slow, giving Lucy too much time to brood over her relationship with Max. If it could be called a relationship. A parting kiss that morning would have been nice, but since he hadn't bothered, he could have at least put an *x* or two or three at the bottom of the note.

After returning from lunch with Katie, Max filled Lucy's thoughts so completely that she scarcely had room to rehash her terrifying experience in the mansion. When she did, the aisles between the rows of books seemed to acquire shadows she'd never before noticed, especially in the basement, where the overflow books were stored. Though she'd left her house without fear, suddenly she felt alone and vulnerable despite her co-workers and the library patrons who came and went.

What would she do if Joe appeared and somehow induced her, against her will, to leave the safety of the library and go with him? Her apprehension grew, until, by the time her shift ended, she was almost afraid to walk home alone.

Reaching her house, she locked herself inside. Where was Max? He'd said that he and Ford would retrieve her car from the mansion, but there was no sign of either Max or her car. She called Ford, but only got his answering machine at home. A deputy at his office told her Ford was in Charleston and wouldn't be back until late.

Just after six a knock at the back door startled Lucy. She knew it couldn't be Max because he'd taken keys. Who was there?

Don't be silly, she chided herself. It's still daylight, and with Max and Ford searching for him, Joe Dooley is hardly going to come knocking at your door. Go answer it.

She felt ashamed of her timidity when she saw Polly waiting to be let in.

"I brought you some fresh-baked butter cookies," Polly said as she sat down at the kitchen table. "They happen to be Max's favorite next to my cocoa drops. He does like chocolate. Never met a man who didn't."

"I guess he's not home yet," Lucy couldn't prevent herself from saying as she dropped onto a chair across from her visitor.

Polly glanced away from her, fastening her gaze on the dishes Lucy had left on the floor for Persy to eat and drink from. "Oh, that cat," she said. "She's such a shameless beggar."

Polly had always been as easy to read as a first-grade primer. Lucy eyed her appraisingly, wondering what was troubling her. Certainly not Persy's behavior. More than likely Max's. Could her neighbor be upset about Max's spending the night there? The thought made Lucy flush. Though she wasn't embarrassed by what she and Max had done—far from it—she hated to cause Polly distress.

"Ford thinks I need protection," she began to explain. "And so—"

Polly cut her off. "Your brother is certainly right." Sitting up straighter, her blue eyes alight with indignation, she said, "With my own eyes I saw Max kiss you in your backyard. To think I approved! At the time I said to myself it might take your mind off losing that shifty-eyed Joe Dooley. I did *not* like him, you know."

"You never mentioned it until this moment," Lucy observed.

"The occasion didn't arise," Polly said. "But, my dear, I quite liked Max. I should have remembered that very few men can be trusted."

"What makes you think Max can't be trusted?"

"I really didn't mean to say anything, but then I decided that after what you went through with Joe Dooley, him turning out to be a criminal and all, it would weigh on my conscience something terrible if I minded my own business the way I was taught to do. I just couldn't bear to see you hurt again."

"I'm not sure I understand," Lucy said slowly.

"I wouldn't want you to think I'm an eavesdropper, because I'd never do such a thing on purpose. But just before noon I was bringing up Max's clean clothes—I wash and dry them for a little extra, you know—when I heard him on the phone talking to that Mina Martin, sounding sweet as sugar. I couldn't believe my ears when he asked her to go out with him."

Lucy stared at Polly with her emotions temporarily in stasis. Max and Mina?

"I can see it comes as a shock, dear," Polly said, "and I'm sorry I had to be the one to break the news. But in the long run it's better to learn sooner than later what kind of a man you're dealing with."

Tamping down the hurt bewilderment that threatened to crush her, Lucy forced a smile. "You're right, of course." She rose from her chair. "Thank you for telling me. And for the cookies."

Polly got up slowly. "I hope I did the right thing. You're sure you don't need to talk about it?"

Lucy shook her head. "It's not that important to me."

After Polly reluctantly took her leave, Lucy relocked the door and retreated to her room, where she stared at the bed and fought back tears. "Damn you, Max," she whispered. "I trusted you."

Driving Lucy's car back from the Franklin mansion, with Mina trailing him in his car, Max tried to understand why his plan had failed.

As soon as he and Mina had passed through the open gates on their way in, he'd sensed Dooley's presence somewhere in the vicinity, though the feeling lessened as they neared the house. So far, so good.

Then Mina's interest in the mansion proved to be far less than her interest in him, especially after he picked the lock so they could enter. She seemed to believe he'd brought her into the house so they could have sex. The very thought made him shudder. He could never make love to anyone in this haunted place, where the faint scent of death still tainted the air.

Being the woman she was, Mina took his reluctance first as a challenge, then as a rejection, stalking out in a huff. A little friendly persuasion sweetened her into strolling through the grounds. Max found the picturesque ruins of an old summerhouse by a stream and made an excuse to leave Mina alone there for more than ten minutes while he set the psychic trap in place. All he accomplished was to annoy her once more; Dooley didn't rise to the bait. Eventually Max gave up.

After parking Lucy's car beside her house, Max slid into his own car to drive Mina home.

"Home!" she exclaimed. "It's not even dark yet. What kind of a date is this anyway?"

"One that failed," he said abruptly, tired of her company, frustrated with his failure and feeling guilty because he'd tried to use Mina without her knowledge. To cap it off, he'd forgotten to unload and defuse the damn carryon at the mansion—it was still locked in the trunk of his car. Though harmless enough there—he wouldn't have let Mina near the car if he didn't think so—he didn't like the idea of her driving around with the damn thing.

"Thanks for bringing my car back to town," he told her.

"If all you wanted was a chauffeur," she snapped, "you should have hired one."

"I'm sorry." No more than the truth. She deserved better than he'd offered her. But he didn't dare to leave Lucy alone with dusk beginning to shadow the earth, so it was impossible to make immediate amends to Mina. "I owe you a dinner in the near future," he told her.

"What makes you think I'll accept?"

He groaned to himself when he heard archness creep back into her voice, preferring her being irritated with him to her being coy.

"The choice is always the woman's," he said gravely, pulling up in front of her apartment with relief.

Before he could move, Mina leaned over and kissed him full on the lips. "Something to remember me by," she said throatily before sliding from the car.

As he drove toward Lucy's, he admitted to himself that last year he'd have found Mina's sexy invitation difficult to resist. Hell, two months ago, even. Now he wasn't even tempted. "Lucy, you little witch," he muttered, "what the devil have you done to me?"

CHAPTER NINE

In Lucy's living room, the phone rang. She started to leave her bedroom, then paused, uncertain whether she wanted to answer it. If Max was the caller she didn't care to talk to him. But was it Max? Ford could be trying to reach her. Or Katie or another one of her friends. On the seventh ring she picked up the phone and said hello.

"Lucy," Joe murmured.

She froze, unable to move or speak.

"You've been a naughty girl, haven't you?" he chided, venom underlying his deceptively silky tone. "You and Ryder. He may think he's won, but he's wrong. He can't win. You're mine. You'll come to me because you have no choice. None at all. Sweet dreams, my bride to be."

Only when he'd ceased talking and hung up was Lucy able to take the phone from her ear. Hugging herself, she retreated to the kitchen, where she stood by the sink, staring unseeingly through the window into the shadows of evening.

She hadn't forgotten about Joe, but in her preoccupation with Max and Mina, his menacing presence had been pushed into the background. Hearing his voice shocked her to the very core of her being, reminding her of the danger lying in wait for her.

There was no question in her mind that he knew she and Max had made love. Not only knew, but was furious with them both. How could he know?

Psychic vampire. She shivered. Where *was* Joe? Had he called from the mansion? Or from somewhere closer? For all she knew he might be on his way to her cottage. What should she do? Panic clogged her throat.

She heard a faint click, as of metal on metal, and bit back a cry. What was it? Since the sound had come from the front of the house, she forced herself to investigate. Anything was better than paralyzed waiting.

As she stepped into the short hall leading to the entry, the front door swung open. Lucy gasped, then all but collapsed in relief when Max walked in. Without thinking, she ran and threw her arms around him. But as he hugged her close, she remembered Mina.

"Let me go!" she cried. When he did, she stepped back quickly.

"I've heard it's a woman's prerogative to change her mind," Max said, raising his permanently quirked left eyebrow higher, "but that had to be the most abrupt change on record. What's wrong?"

"Joe called me."

"When?"

"Shortly before you arrived."

He strode past her to the phone and fiddled with the Caller ID Ford had attached to it the day after Max had moved into Polly's.

"Lucy," Joe's voice said again, making her cringe. She longed to stop her ears as the recording played back. His words were even more frightening the second time around.

Max cursed as he shut off the machine.

"I feel as if he's hiding somewhere outside watching me," she said.

"He's not that close," Max assured her. Taking keys from his pocket, he dropped them on the coffee table. "I brought your car back."

She decided not to let on that earlier she'd heard a car in the driveway and looked from her bedroom window in time to see him get out of her vehicle and join Mina in his. "Thank you," she said curtly.

"The necklace wasn't inside the car," he added.

For an instant she didn't pick up on his meaning, then she recalled that horrible moment when she'd discovered she was wearing the bridal necklace that Joe had given her. "I'm almost positive I took it off in my car," she said.

"Chances are Dooley found the necklace," Max told her, "and that's bad news. He'll try to use it to summon you, and unfortunately, since you wore it so recently, the necklace carries enough of your essence to be of help to him."

She stared at him in consternation, waiting for him to assure her that he could thwart Joe. When he didn't, she swallowed convulsively, remembering all too well how she'd been forced by Joe to drive to the mansion against her will—or rather without any will at all.

"I can't block his summons," Max said, "but if I stay with you constantly I'll be able to prevent you from answering the call."

"How can he do all these horrible things?" she cried.

"He's powerful. Those among us who choose the wrong side, the dark side, often gain tremendous power before being destroyed by it."

"You said he wasn't really Joe Dooley. Who is he?"

"As far as I know he's a man named Judson Ingalls—at least, that was the name he used when I first came in contact with him. It's possible that's not his real name any more than Dooley is. If it's to his advantage, he assumes the name of his most recent victim. In this case, he passed himself off as Dooley in order to claim the Franklin estate."

"He said he was Letitia Franklin's nephew," Lucy said, grimacing as she recalled how eagerly she'd accepted Joe's lies.

"The real Joseph R. Dooley is—or was—Miss Franklin's nephew. I believe that the vampire brought the real nephew with him to the mansion, deliberately keeping him alive as a prisoner in the tower until he could be certain he no longer needed Dooley."

"That horrible smell—" Lucy paused, sickened, and put her hand over her mouth.

"Yes, Dooley was dead by the time you were summoned to the mansion, but his body was still in the tower. The vampire must have disposed of the body after I rescued you, because I noticed today that the stink is almost gone from the house."

After taking a moment to recover, Lucy asked, "You were after him because of Joseph R. Dooley?"

Max shook his head. "Not merely Dooley. I've been after him for years. Dooley was his seventh victim, my sister was his first." Pain twisted his face. "Or at least the first victim I knew of."

Her impulse to ease his pain made Lucy touch his arm in sympathy. "Come into the kitchen," she said. "I'll make coffee."

"Coffee, the universal panacea."

The words were innocuous enough, but his voice was strained, as though the anguish over his sister's death lurked just below the surface.

"Thanks."

Polly's cookies were still on the table and, as he drank the coffee, he began to eat them, one after another, almost as if unaware of what he was doing. Finally he pushed the plate with the few remaining cookies on it away and shook his head to more coffee.

"Olivia was my twin," he said, staring into the dregs of his coffee rather than looking at her. "Because we were both aberrants we were even closer than most twins. I was away when she met the vampire, away when he used his power to control her. When I returned, I sensed the evil in him, but I didn't know enough then to realize what he was or what desperate danger she was in. Olivia refused to heed my warning to be careful, to go slow. I didn't understand that by then she had no free choice. When I persisted, she ran off with him."

Max took a deep, shuddering breath. "During my search for her, I could sense her increasing terror, but—" He shook his head. "I found her too late."

Lucy cringed from imagining what horrors Olivia had gone through and concentrated on her sympathy for Max. Before she could tell him how sorry she was, he went on with his story.

"I've hunted for the bastard ever since, finding his other victims along the way but never him—until I caught up with him in St. John's Church. You know what's happened since."

Suddenly Max slammed his fist down on the table, startling Lucy and making the dishes jump.

"Hear me, you damned vampire! This time you lose. I win."

He got to his feet, strode to the back door, unlocked it, called "I'll be back" over his shoulder and plunged into the deepening dusk.

When he returned through the same door soon afterward, he was carrying Persy under one arm and a small black case in his hand. "She sleeps with us," he announced.

"Us?" Lucy echoed, having had time to remember about Mina.

"Surely you don't object to having a cat in your bed."

"I wasn't referring to the cat," she said tartly. "Persy is welcome in my bed."

"But I'm not?" He scowled. "What the hell's wrong with you all of a sudden?"

"Nothing."

"When a woman says nothing she means everything."

She glared at him without replying.

He raised his eyebrows. "Having second thoughts about last night, are you?"

"Second, third and fourth."

"It's too late."

"I don't care to discuss this further," she said.

Max eyed her levelly, noting the stubborn set of her chin. Dividing forces was definitely not a good idea—they needed to remain close both physically and psychically—but in her present mood he knew she wouldn't listen to reason. She obviously had no intention of telling him what was bugging her. He felt no taint of evil, so she wasn't being influenced by the vampire. What was it?

Noticing a few cookies still remained on the table, he reached for one—he'd skipped dinner and was still hungry. Given her mind-set, though, Lucy wasn't likely to offer him a meal.

"These taste like the ones Polly bakes," he remarked.

"That's because they are," Lucy snapped.

So Polly had been here while he was at the mansion. Was that significant? Probably. Despite all her protestations to the contrary, Polly loved to gossip. What might she have said to upset Lucy?

After a moment he nodded. Polly had almost certainly overheard his phone call to Mina and probably had told Lucy, who wouldn't have understood his reason for making the call to Mina.

"You didn't expect me to use *you* as bait, did you?" he demanded. "That would have been far too dangerous."

Lucy blinked, clearly confused. He waited, wondering how long it would take her to see through his words to the issue underneath, the one bothering her.

"Bait?" she said cautiously. "You mean to lure the vampire into the open?"

"He's somewhere in the vicinity of the mansion, and I hoped to trap him." Again he waited for her to digest what he'd said.

"But you didn't."

"No, I failed. As he told you. He's hungry, but apparently not desperate enough to let his hunger lead him into danger."

"Are you telling me you used Mina as bait?" Lucy's tone was incredulous. "I don't believe that."

"I'm not proud of it. I had no right to expose her to danger without her knowledge."

"True," Lucy said coldly. "Quite possibly she wouldn't have let you kiss her if she'd known."

Damn, he thought he'd wiped all the lipstick off, he must have missed a spot. "I don't claim it was the best idea I ever had," he said defensively, "but I figured there was a chance I might trap him."

Persy wriggled loose from Max's arms, jumped onto the counter by the sink, put her paws on the windowsill and gazed into the darkness. Watching her, Max tensed, then probed for the vampire's alien presence.

"Is he out there?" Lucy whispered.

"Not close enough for me to sense," Max replied. "The cat may be reacting to something else."

As he spoke, Persy lost interest in whatever was outside the window, turned and leaped from the counter to the floor. She gave the empty food dish a tentative sniff, lapped some water, then left the kitchen.

"Safe for the moment," Max said. "If you're over your twinge of jealousy, maybe we can discuss what's really important."

Lucy glared at him. "What do you mean jealousy? *You* were the one who spoke about eternal bonding, not me. I have absolutely no reason to be jealous."

"No reason at all. We're bonded."

"Whatever that means."

With some effort, Max checked his rising annoyance. "Sit down, Lucy," he said as evenly as he could.

She raised her chin defiantly, stalked from the kitchen into the living room and perched on the arm of one of the chairs.

He followed her, sat in the chair she'd chosen and, before she could get away, pulled her down onto his lap and kissed her. Ignoring her squirming, he deepened the kiss, at the same time striving to reach her psychically. The moment he found himself wrapped in her glow, she stopped struggling, not only yielding to his caresses but responding so ardently he had difficulty in controlling his urge to carry her into the bedroom and go on from there.

Summoning his rapidly diminishing willpower, he managed to take his lips from hers. "That's part of what the bonding means," he murmured.

She sighed. "It felt wonderful, as though I were wrapped in warmth and light."

"You were and so was I. We create the glowing light between us. Why would I ever want to kiss another woman, Lucy, when this can happen only with you?"

She gazed at him solemnly for long moments, finally offering a reluctant smile. He hugged her, rose to his feet with her in his arms and deposited her on one end of the couch. He sat at the other end.

"I can't concentrate on anything but making love when you're in my arms," he said. "Meanwhile he's prowling the darkness and we need all the ammunition we can conjure up. Think back, Lucy. When you were out of your body, I showed you an image that dispelled Shuck. What did that image mean to you?''

She frowned and sat up straighter, tucking her feet under her. ''The moon? No, more like a moonstone. I thought of my grandmother's moonstone necklace.''

''Where is it?''

''In my bedroom. She bequeathed it to me before she died.''

''Have you ever worn the necklace?''

Lucy nodded. ''At what was supposed to be my wedding in St. John's. The necklace fell off.''

''You didn't wear it as a child?''

''No, because the clasp was broken.'' Lucy hesitated, finally adding, ''But something did happen the night after my ninth birthday party. I'd put the necklace on my bedside stand and I had a bad dream.'' Honesty forced her to revise what she'd said. ''It was a vision, a terrible vision.''

With some reluctance, she went on to tell him what had happened.

After a short silence, Max asked, ''So the necklace was close to you when you had your vision of your parents' death?''

''Yes. I put it away after that.''

Max leaned toward her, his face intent.

''Why?''

''I don't know, I guess I feared the moonstones had something to do with what happened to my parents.''

''So when you put the necklace away, you stopped seeing things?'' Max asked.

"I didn't connect one with the other until now."

"The necklace seems to influence you. If you were wearing it when you saw past the facade of the man who calls himself Joe Dooley, it could have been the moonstones that allowed you to glimpse his unclean spirit."

Lucy shook her head. "I wasn't wearing the moonstones, but I did have the necklace with me because I was taking it to the jewelry shop to have the clasp repaired."

"Any particular reason you decided to resurrect the necklace?"

"Actually, Grandma told me to in a dream. Or maybe she really did appear to me—I'm not certain any more of what's real and what isn't."

He reached over and touched her hand. "I'm real. You're real. What we share is real. Unfortunately, the vampire is also a reality. I want you to put on the moonstone necklace. Now."

Lucy bit her lip. "I'm afraid of what I'll see."

"Don't be. Whatever vision you may have can't be worse than what that bastard has already put you through. Think of it this way—what you see may help us to win."

Once she agreed, Max trailed her into the bedroom, where Persy was curled asleep in the exact center of her bed. He watched Lucy pick the moonstone necklace from the dresser, place it around her neck and fumble with the clasp.

"Let me," he said, coming up behind her. She relinquished the clasp and he discovered how unusual the mechanism was, not at all easy to put together. "Tricky," he muttered.

"The jeweler wanted to put a new clasp on instead of repairing this one," she said, "but I wasn't sure Grandma would approve."

"There, I've got it," he said. "I hope the necklace unclasps easier than this."

"Much easier. Sometimes by itself." She fingered the moonstones. "I've always liked to touch them." Glancing in the mirror above the dressing table, she said, "I'm not too sure they go with cutoffs and a T-shirt, though."

Noticing how the slight glow that always surrounded Lucy had brightened and expanded, Max said, "Maybe not, but they certainly suit *you*."

"At least nothing's happening this time. I mean, so far I'm not having any visions. Did you think I would?"

"I don't know what to expect, though I believe it's important for you to keep the moonstones always near you."

"I'm sure you hoped I'd have a vision."

"Foreseeing isn't an exact talent," he told her. "Most often the visions are random and, though true, sometimes inexplicable. And they can't be summoned to order. I could compare them to a wild card in poker—you never know when one will turn up, but when it does you may come out a winner."

Easing onto the bed, he stretched out and lifted Persy onto his stomach before glancing at her with a question in his eyes. Did she still object to sharing her bed with him?

"If you think I'm sleeping on the couch you're badly mistaken," she told him.

"Does that mean I have to?" he asked.

"I wouldn't be able to sleep a wink if you did," she admitted. "Not with *him* haunting the darkness."

Considerably relieved, he said, "If we're together, I can set wards so we can sleep with some degree of safety, but the bonding that would happen if we made love transcends all wards, leaving us vulnerable. So no lovemaking." He smiled wryly. "With us in the same bed that's a hell of a lot easier said than done."

"I hope you don't want me to wear the moonstones to bed," Lucy said.

"No. But lay the necklace on the nightstand, within reach." Max set the cat aside, rose and left the room. He returned with the small case he'd carried in earlier.

Lucy watched, fascinated, as he opened the case and removed a white candle, which he fitted into a copper holder and placed on her dresser. Clearing a space beside the candle, he set out various small, capped jars. He then pulled the head of the bed away from the wall, far enough for a narrow passageway between bed and wall.

She didn't understand the words of the chant he used as he sprinkled small amounts of dried plants around the bed, while a scent both aromatic and spicy filled the room. Persy observed his movements with as much interest as Lucy.

When he was done, he placed everything back in the case except the candle and its holder. Approaching Lucy, he ran his hands through her hair, leaving a pleasant aroma but nothing else tangible behind when he'd finished. He did the same with Persy's fur. The cat apparently approved, because she didn't immediately begin washing herself.

Later, when they were in bed with the lights out, he said, "Mina kissed me, not the other way around."

Lucy smiled in the darkness. "Excuses, excuses," she said. "Like Adam did to Eve, men always blame the woman."

"Much as I wanted to, I sure as hell didn't seduce you last night," he said. "If you recall it was the other way around."

"Somehow I knew it was the right time." Her tone carried a tinge of defensiveness.

"So you said. And in at least one way, it was. You upset the vampire's plans or he wouldn't have phoned to threaten you. I know the call frightened you, but the fact he made it shows he's vulnerable. As for our bonding—"

He paused and she heard him sigh.

"Ah, Lucy, do you have any idea just how much I want you?"

His words sent a fiery tingle through her. "Some idea," she admitted, knowing she felt the same need. If she moved no more than a few inches she'd be snuggled against him. How she longed to feel his solid warmth against her body.

Persy, curled up near her feet, roused and crawled up between her and Max, there settling down to sleep.

"Our feline chaperon," he said, amusement in his voice. "Persy is clearly a female who knows males can't be trusted."

"More than that," Lucy said ruefully, "she knows from her own experience that females can't be trusted, either."

"I'd kiss you good-night if I thought I could keep to one kiss," he said softly.

"Let's stick to words. Good night, Max."

"Good night, my—" His pause was brief. "Lucy."

What had he been going to say? she wondered. My what? Darling? Dear? Or maybe—my love? A thrill whispered through her as she realized how much she wanted to hear those words from him. And say them in return.

But now wasn't the time. Not with the dreadful creature he called a psychic vampire stalking her. She tried not to relive those terrible minutes in the mansion when the vampire had summoned her, forcing her to climb the tower stairs against her will, while the real Joe Dooley lay dead beside him.

Max had saved her from a horrible fate. She hoped that his sister hadn't had to suffer for days on end the way poor Joe Dooley must have.

And to think she'd almost married this hideous vampire! Never mind how he looked on the outside or who she'd believed him to be; her vision had shown her the truth the moment they'd met. Why hadn't she trusted her own insight? How could she ever have been so blind as to believe his lying words?

Her grandmother had tried to warn her, but she hadn't understood the complete message. Reaching toward the bedside stand, she touched the moonstones. Almost instantly her mind quieted and her eyelids drooped shut.

Sometime later Lucy awoke with a start, aware even before she could think clearly that something was wrong. Persy, crouched next to her, growled deep in her throat, and though Max didn't move, Lucy could feel his tension as if it were her own.

"Max?" she said softly.

"Shh," he warned.

She heard nothing, but she could sense the evil seeping through the walls of the bedroom from outside and her heart began to pound in fright.

"Take my hand," Max whispered in her ear, "and don't let go. When I get up, you get up with me. I put two lighters near the candle, one on each side. When we reach the dresser, pick up one of the lighters with your free hand. We must light the candle together, our flames mingling." His hand closed around hers.

She obeyed him to the letter. Her hand trembled as she flicked the lighter, and for an instant she feared she couldn't make it work. When it flared, the flame wavered precariously but didn't go out as she joined it to Max's flame at the white candle's wick. A symbol, she thought when the wick caught. A symbol of our bonding.

A powerful symbol, her grandmother's voice said in her mind. *Such a bond is a tie that evil cannot sever, an unbreakable link.*

Lucy stared at the yellow flame of the candle until Max gave a gentle tug at her hand, leading her back to the bed. As they climbed in, she realized she no longer sensed evil. Together they'd banished the vampire.

But for how long?

CHAPTER TEN

In the morning, the phone woke Lucy, but before she managed to get her feet on the floor, Max was already halfway to the bedroom door.

"I'll get it," he told her.

Because the vampire might be the caller, she knew. God knows she didn't ever want to hear that silky, menacing voice again. But if someone else was calling, Max answering her phone would be an item of gossip in no time at all. Lucy decided she didn't much care. She stood up, stretched and sauntered from the bedroom.

"She's in good shape," Max was saying as she came into the living room. "He's definitely after her, though. I'm camping here until I nail him."

Lucy realized he must be talking to Ford.

After a pause Max said, "He'll have to get past me first and that's not likely to happen. Thanks for running down the phone number. I figured it was a pay phone, but the location confirms my feeling that he's not going far from the mansion."

When he hung up, Max said, "Your brother."

"I figured," Lucy said. "He doesn't mind that you're staying here?"

"He didn't seem to."

Lucy raised her eyebrows, hardly able to believe her overprotective brother didn't object to Max's spending nights in her cottage.

"You notice I used the the word 'camping,'" Max said. "I don't want to get him riled up. With the vampire still on the loose I don't need Maguire down my throat, as well. He traced your call last night to a pay phone at a gas station not far from the Franklin mansion."

His gaze fastened on her, taking in the extra large T-shirt she'd worn to sleep in. "I don't know how anything so voluminous can be so sexy," he said. "Maybe because I keep being tempted to find out if you've got anything on underneath."

She was equally tempted to let him try, but Persy had other plans. The cat's persistent weaving around Lucy's ankles, accompanied by plaintive pleas to be fed, couldn't be ignored.

Max shrugged. "I'll shower while you deal with our watchcat."

Once she'd eaten, Persy wanted to go out. After closing and relocking the door behind her, Lucy returned to the bedroom. Conscious of the water running in the bathroom, she paused outside the door and tried to picture Max in the shower, but her image of him was fuzzy because she had yet to see him totally naked. She'd never taken a shower with a man, but why not? With her hand on the doorknob, Lucy hesitated, remembering how the vampire had sensed the one time she'd made love with Max. If they made love again, he might also know and somehow take advantage of the situation.

Sighing, she took her hand off the knob and went into her bedroom. Noticing the moonstone necklace had been knocked off the bedside stand, she bent and picked it up, running the gems through her fingers. Did the necklace really trigger visions? She'd worn it the previous evening without any such result.

Lucy was about to replace the moonstones on the stand, when a sudden attack of giddiness made her stumble against the bed and then the room faded from her sight....

Where was she? Not in her cottage, nor any other familiar place. A faint reddish light barely illuminated the darkness. She stood beside a brass bed with a plush velvet covering. Floor-to-ceiling windows with walnut paneling between them surrounded her. Beyond the windows the blackness of night hid the view until a flash of lightning revealed how high up in the air she was. As thunder rumbled, she realized what she'd seen and she clutched the necklace so tightly the metal clasp hurt her hands. She was in the tower room of the mansion!

And she was not alone.

Rain slashed against the windows, the wind howled. The tower smelled of age, of mold and of death. Across the room from her, two shadowy figures grappled by one of the long windows, two men in a violent struggle, a fight to the death, she knew. And her life depended on the outcome.

The red glow was too dim for her to identify the men, but, aware of the feel of evil, she knew one of them must be the vampire. The next lightning flash showed her the face of the other man. She gasped.

Max!

In the blinding darkness following the brilliance of the lightning, the two men once again became mere shadows, their identity lost. As they battled on, she couldn't tell which one was Max, so there was no way to discover who might be winning.

Evil thickened the air, lapping at her as though Shuck himself were there in the room, licking her with his ghastly tongue. Though she tried to move she could not; she was frozen in place, unable to creep closer to see who was Max and to try to help him if she could.

All she could do was watch apprehensively as the shadowy figures grappled and broke apart, only to come at each other again. The storm battered the tower, thunder growled, drowning any sounds the fighters might be making.

One of the men threw the other against one of the windows, shattering it. Would he fall through? She held her breath, not knowing who he was. As rain blew in through the broken window, he stumbled to his feet, away from the danger.

The other man leaped on him, battering him to the floor. With a cry of triumph, the man still on his feet grasped the fallen man, lifting him in his arms, while she gaped in shock. How could any man be so strong?

As the winner staggered toward the broken window with his burden, she fought to break the paralysis holding her helpless. She failed. The flash of lightning she'd been praying for blazed across the room. By its glare she saw the vampire at the broken window raise Max's limp body high.

"No!" she screamed, knowing her protest was futile. Nothing could stop the horrible monster from flinging Max to his death far below.

At that moment her paralysis lifted—but too late, far too late. And then everything went black.

Max, fresh from the shower, was toweling himself dry when he heard Lucy scream. Dropping the towel, he raced from the bathroom. To his dismay, he found her sprawled unconscious on the floor near the bed. As he gathered her into his arms and lifted her onto the bed, he saw the moonstone necklace wrapped around one of her hands and he breathed a bit easier.

He'd been afraid the vampire had somehow bypassed his wards and reached her, but now he discarded his fear, aware that visions sometimes affected the seers so strongly they passed out.

He removed the necklace from her hand and put it on the nightstand. Easing onto the bed beside her, he pulled her into his arms, knowing she needed to refuel her psychic energy. Since they now shared a permanent psychic bond, if he gathered her close to him, Lucy, even though unconscious, could tap into his energy and take what she needed.

Holding her tenderly, he gazed into her still face with what he tried to think of as affectionate concern. But he'd never been able to lie successfully to himself and he knew in his heart the feeling consuming him was far more, though he refused to put a name to it.

How lovely she was, both in her outer form and inwardly, as well—the most beautiful woman he'd ever known. He leaned to her and brushed his lips gently over hers. "Lucy," he whispered. "Lucy, Lucy."

She stirred in his grasp; her eyelids fluttered and then opened. For a long moment she lay still, staring unbelievingly at him, her lips soundlessly forming his name. At last she moved, clutching at him fiercely.

"You can't die. I won't let you die!" she cried. "Never!"

His blood ran cold. What had she seen in her vision?

Tears welled in her eyes and ran down her cheeks. "Max, Max, I can't believe you're really here with me. Hold me, never let me go."

Making an effort, he put his concern over her vision aside. "I can't think of anything I'd rather do than hold you," he murmured soothingly, stroking her back.

Though he meant to offer no more than comforting closeness, his body betrayed him. As he fought to ignore his escalating desire, her sobs lessened, then stopped. She sighed and snuggled closer, only to pull back and look at him.

"You're naked!" she exclaimed. And smiled.

The smile was his undoing. Moments later her T-shirt and the panties she wore underneath were on the floor and he was kissing her with all the pent-up passion he'd tried to shelve.

Intoxicated by her scent and taste and by the arousing sensation of her skin against his, he groaned in pleasure, his need blazing completely out of control. The intensity of his physical passion surpassed, for the moment, the exquisite blending of her psychic energy with his.

"My love, my love," he murmured as he eased inside her, not aware of what he'd said or how much it revealed.

Joined in a complete, magical union of body and spirit, he traveled with her through every nuance of pleasure until they could go no higher. A violent surge of consummation blazed through them at the same moment, enhanced by each knowing what the other felt.

Much later, lying in the bed with Lucy in his arms, Max reluctantly returned to the here and now. Raising onto one elbow, he said. "I know the moonstones triggered a vision. Tell me what you saw."

She swallowed and he felt her tense.

"It couldn't have been a true vision," she protested.

"True or not, I want to hear about it."

"Please, Max, I don't want to remember."

"There's no choice."

She freed herself from his arms and propped her pillow against the headboard, pulling up the sheet to cover her breasts, shielding her lovely body from his gaze. Not from shyness, he decided, but defensively, and not so much a shield against him as against the vision.

"I was in a place I've never visited before," she began. "A place I never wanted to visit—the tower of the Franklin mansion. It was night. You were there and so was he—the vampire. Outside a storm raged. Inside—" She paused and bit her lip.

"Tell me about inside," he said encouragingly. "What happened?"

Her face paled, her teeth clenched and she shuddered. "He won," she whispered.

No matter how hard he tried, Max was unable to coax any details from her.

"I can't talk about it" was all she would say, over and over.

When she left the bed to take a shower and dress, Max, still propped against the headboard, pondered the first words she'd uttered when she recovered from the vision: *You can't die. I won't let you die.* And she'd ended her story with *He won.* He took a deep breath and let it out slowly. Visions seen by someone as powerful as Lucy ran true.

Springing from the bed, he strode to the window, pulled the curtain aside and stared into the brightness of a day warmed by sunshine. Life was good, even wonderful, at least lately. Death was final. And one of them, either he or the vampire, must die.

"Hear me, Vampire," he muttered. "If I go, I take you with me."

In the early afternoon, Max made what he told Lucy would be a hurried trip to Polly's to collect clean clothes. Lucy had been quiet all day, brooding over her vision and trying to convince herself it couldn't possibly have been a true one.

Yet the visions she'd seen had always been true. Her parents' death. Joe Dooley as Dracula. Her blighted wedding bouquet. Max's anguished face when he was caught in the vampire's trap. True, one and all.

Except for the strange vision she'd had of Luke Cassidy in St. John's Church after Max had entered and Joe had fled—could that have been true? Luke had been sitting in a pew with his son in his lap. Katie had been walking with her, leading her to the back of the church. She'd sensed Katie's distress and somehow knew it had to do with Luke. At that moment

Luke had changed to a total stranger, to a man she'd never seen before. The boy on his lap had remained the same. And then, as suddenly as he'd changed, Luke was himself again.

Surely it had been a vision that made no sense at all. A false vision? It had to be. And if she'd seen one false vision, it meant her visions weren't all true.

Max mustn't die. She loved him with all her heart and soul, with everything she was. She sighed, remembering how he'd murmured "my love" during their lovemaking. Was she his love as he was hers?

He couldn't die! Yet if her vision was true, he would. And she had no way to save him.

Lucy raised her chin. The vision had to be false; that was all there was to it. She'd prove her case right this minute by calling up Luke Cassidy and asking him a few questions.

Once she heard his voice on the other end of the line, though, Lucy lost her nerve. How could she possibly explain this over the phone? He'd think she was crazy. She'd have to talk to him in person. But where?

Thinking quickly, she asked, "Do you have time to meet me at the library around four this afternoon? There's something I have to discuss with you, and I don't feel comfortable doing it on the phone. I won't take much time."

After an initial hesitation, Luke agreed, and she hung up just as Max entered the kitchen through the back door.

"Polly scolded me," he said as he joined her in the living room. "She told me I shouldn't be fooling around with a nice girl like you—or words to that effect."

Lucy smiled to herself. How like Polly. "What did you say?"

"That nice girls were the only kind I ever fooled around with."

"You didn't."

He grinned. "What I actually said was that your brother had appointed me as your bodyguard because Dooley was still in the area. And because I was guarding you, I had to stay with you at all times. Polly agreed guarding you was a full-time job. It seems Dooley was never her choice for your husband."

"So she said." Lucy glanced at her watch. "As my bodyguard, I guess you'll be coming to the library with me in about an hour, then."

"I thought you weren't working today."

"I promised Ada I'd take over for her from three to four so she wouldn't have to change her dental appointment." Which was why she'd asked Luke to meet her there.

She saw no reason to mention setting up the meeting to Max because she didn't want him asking a lot of questions she wasn't ready to answer. If he believed Luke was at the library merely as a patron he'd think nothing of it if he happened to see them talking.

When Luke arrived at exactly four, Lucy asked him to wait for her in the local reference room, a glassed-in area open to patrons only with prior approval by a member of the library staff. She handed Luke the small green card that would gain him entry and waited impatiently for Ada's return.

Five minutes later, Ada arrived and took over at the desk. As Lucy hurried toward the reference room, she glanced around, looking for Max, but he was nowhere in sight. She let herself into the room and joined Luke at a table, sitting across from him. He closed the "Clover in 1850" booklet he'd been reading and gave her a level look.

"What's this all about, Lucy?" he asked.

"Something strange happened in the church on my supposed-to-be wedding day," she began, going on to explain to him what she'd seen when she'd looked at him. "It was a reoccurrence of the visions that began when I was a child," she said. "Some of them are true visions, but obviously the one of you couldn't have been."

Luke took a deep breath. "Let's see if I have this right. You asked me here to find out if you had a true vision when you looked at me in St. John's Church some weeks ago. Your vision was that I changed into another man. Would you mind describing him?"

Taken aback, Lucy dredged her memory and came up with a somewhat sketchy description for Luke. He nodded, his face expressionless. She waited expectantly, but he didn't speak.

Growing edgy, she finally said, "A false vision, right?"

He sighed. "I'm afraid not, Lucy."

Standing near the library's three computers, Max had a clear view through the glass partition enclosing the reference room, where Lucy sat at a table, facing a man. He'd already asked a patron and discovered what the man's name was—Luke Cassidy. It didn't ring a bell.

What the devil was Lucy doing in there with him? It was obviously a setup, because she'd first sent Cassidy into the room and then joined him as soon as she was free to leave the desk. It was also obvious that she didn't like what he was saying to her.

Why hadn't she told Max she was meeting Cassidy? Something he refused to acknowledge as jealousy gnawed at him as he stared at them. Cassidy was a good-looking bastard, no getting around it. A former boyfriend?

Lucy pushed her chair back and rose, followed by Cassidy, who came around the table to stand beside her. Lucy gazed earnestly into his face, offering her hand as she spoke to him. Cassidy took her hand, holding it for longer than Max liked before letting go. Then they both headed for the door.

Max ducked out of sight, peering cautiously from between two stacks as the two of them left the room. Cassidy strode toward the library entrance, but Lucy paused, glancing around. Looking for me, Max told himself. Probably wondering if I noticed anything.

He emerged from between the stacks and sauntered over to her. ''Ready to go?'' he asked.

She nodded without smiling and he could feel her distress. What had that bastard done to upset her? And why the devil had she kept her meeting with Cassidy a secret?

As they left the library, Max noticed the sun was hidden by dirty-gray clouds, lowering clouds that promised rain, and soon. As though affected by the dreariness, they walked back to her cottage in gloomy silence.

When they reached the front door, Max said, ''I forgot to mention that Polly's sending over a platter of fried chicken for our evening meal. 'Lucy's looking puny lately,' she told me. 'You make it your business to see that she eats right.' ''

"I'm not very hungry." Lucy felt dispirited.

Max inserted the two keys, unlocking the door. "Then I guess I'll have to feed you," he said as he ushered her inside. "Bodyguards can't have their clients turning puny on them."

Her smile was a feeble imitation of the real thing. He relocked the door, grabbed her upper arms and swung her around to face him. "What the hell's bugging you? And don't tell me nothing is. I already know that's a lie."

She stared at the floor. "I'm tired."

"You probably are. But you're also evading my question." He gave her a little shake. "Damn it, look at me!"

When she did, her changeable eyes held so much grief that he felt a tug at his heart. Almost immediately this tender feeling was superseded by a spurt of anger at Cassidy.

"What the devil did he tell you that hurt so much?" he demanded.

She blinked, her expression becoming more animated, if only with annoyance. "I should have known you'd be spying on me," she accused, pulling away from him.

"That's my job and you know it. Come on, out with it."

Lucy folded her arms across her breasts and frowned at him. "No. I won't tell you. I promised Luke I wouldn't tell anyone. It's his secret, not mine."

"If it's Cassidy's secret, why are *you* upset?"

"I'm not upset about his secret."

Her face crumpled and she burst into tears, turning from him and running into the bedroom. He heard the door slam shut.

Didn't she understand yet that he couldn't be shut away from her? Not by her stubbornness or by outside influences or by closed doors. He started for the bedroom, stopping short before he got there.

Cool down, Ryder, he advised himself. Let her cry for a while; she'll feel better. She's safe enough on her bed with the wards all around.

He did have a job to do, one he'd been putting off. That damn booby-trapped carryon of Lucy's was still in the trunk of his car. It was past time he removed the thing and defused it. His mind made up, he left the cottage, retrieved the bag and carried it, still by the wire hanger, to a patch of dying weeds near the shed. Being the most unattractive place in Lucy's yard, the spot seemed appropriate.

Aware of how to begin the defusing, Max set about the process methodically, careful to overlook nothing. He sure as hell didn't intend to be caught in one of the vampire's psychic traps again. Undoing was trickier than doing, especially if the trap had been set by someone else. First came the scan, then an extremely cautious probe to determine if you'd interpreted the scan correctly.

Max breathed a sigh of relief when scan and probe were finished. Now he knew exactly what had to be done. Unfortunately it was energy consuming, but he had time to renew his energy before nightfall. Night was the natural haunt of the vampire, so he felt safe enough at the moment.

Before he finished, a drizzle began. He ignored the thin rain, concentrating completely on his task. He found himself soaked through when at last the trap had been completely dispersed. Since the bag was now as harmless as it looked, he carried it back to the cottage with him, using the handles this time.

Lucy was sitting in the kitchen with a cup of tea in front of her.

"What happened to the coffee?" he asked.

"I ran out. It's tea or nothing." She sounded almost normal.

He held up the bag. "I didn't get around to giving this back to you."

She stared at the wet carryon suspiciously. "Where did you find it?"

"In a motel. Don't worry, I wouldn't let you have the bag if I wasn't positive nothing about it could harm you."

She gestured toward the accordion door that hid the washer-and-dryer alcove. "Thanks, but I think I'll wash everything inside the bag anyway."

He nodded and set the carryon inside the alcove, noticing for the first time that the oven was on and the kitchen smelled deliciously of chicken. Polly must have brought dinner over while he was working by the shed. Good thing—he was starved.

"Do I have time to change into dry clothes before we eat?" he asked.

"If you hurry. I've been waiting for you to come in and feed me as you promised," she said with a sly glance at him.

He grinned at her as he left the kitchen, elated at her change of mood. Sooner or later he'd discover what had troubled her, but for now he'd let things ride.

After the meal, his depletion of energy caught up with him, and without meaning to, he dozed in a living room chair while Lucy started the washer.

He was shocked awake by a caterwaul. Lucy had already flicked on the back light and was unlocking the door when he ran into the kitchen. "Persy!" she cried. "She's in trouble."

Max grabbed the flashlight Lucy kept in the catch-all drawer and plunged into the darkness with her at his heels. They found Persy huddled under the lounge. Scattered feathers told Max what had happened—the owl had swooped at the cat and found an opponent he couldn't conquer.

"She's hurt," Lucy said after he'd lifted the chair and set it down away from the cat. "In this light I can't tell how badly. I'm afraid if I pick her up I'll make things worse."

Max stripped off his T-shirt, laid it on the ground with one edge tucked slightly under the cat, then gently eased Persy onto the shirt. "I warned you to beware of those other night hunters," he told her as he lifted cat and shirt onto one of the lounge cushions so he could carry her into the house with the least damage possible.

Once inside, at Lucy's direction he set cushion and cat on the kitchen table. Three long, bloody furrows along Persy's side showed how the owl's talons had gripped her. Luckily the furrows seemed relatively shallow. Max could find no other obvious injuries but it was clear the cat was in pain.

"There's no vet in town," Lucy said, "but there's one on the road between Clover and Riverville." As she spoke, she ran her hand gently along Persy's body. Suddenly she stopped and looked up at Max. "I'm not sure, but I think maybe she's about to have her kittens."

At the same moment, Max sensed the vampire.

CHAPTER ELEVEN

Lucy, her concern focused on Persy, didn't at first notice that Max was no longer at her side. Though the gouges along Persy's side were no longer bleeding, Lucy worried that the strain of the kittens coming might make the injury worse.

She counted back to when the toms had been yowling and fighting in her backyard, then tried to remember what a cat's gestation period normally was. She came to the conclusion it was possibly a bit too early for Persy to be having her kittens.

"Maybe we ought to take her to a vet," Lucy said. When Max didn't answer, she looked toward where he'd been. Finding him gone, she glanced around the kitchen.

To her surprise, because he was ordinarily so careful to keep the doors locked, especially at night, she saw he stood in the open back door, staring into the darkness.

"Max?" she said.

He ignored her.

She raised her voice. "Max!"

Without turning, he said, "Find a box for Persy and take her into your bedroom. Place the box on your bed, put on the moonstone necklace and stay on the bed with the cat."

She was about to ask questions, when he ordered, "Do it now!"

Alarmed by the tenseness in his voice, she stared at him. What was out there? Persy growled deep in her throat and Lucy switched her attention back to the cat. Persy's growling continued, convincing Lucy that both Max and the cat sensed danger, even though she did not. For the cat's sake, she'd best do as Max told her.

Remembering the box for storing extra cleaning supplies that sat on the floor of her small pantry, she crossed the room, dumped everything from the box, grabbed the old sheet she'd left there to be torn into dust cloths and lined the bottom of the box with it.

Returning to the cat, she lifted Persy very carefully into the box, picked up cat and box and, with one last look at Max, hurried to her bedroom.

Sitting cross-legged on her bed with the box in front of her, she struggled to fasten the necklace around her neck, even though she feared she might have a vision. She trusted Max; he wouldn't tell her to wear the moonstones if there wasn't a reason.

Once Lucy had fastened the clasp, instead of the momentary dizziness that sometimes preceded a vision, she felt an unusual calmness settle over her. As though Persy also felt its soothing presence, the cat stopped growling. Lucy watched her hunch up, and in a matter of minutes, a tiny head appeared at the opening of the cat's birth canal.

Persy expelled the kitten with no apparent effort and immediately set about licking it clean, biting through the umbilical cord and then eating the nourishing afterbirth.

Lucy had seen newborn kittens before, so she knew how helpless and naked they looked. But this one seemed smaller than any she remembered and she watched it anxiously. Would the kitten survive? Fear crawled through her. The kitten had to live! It was of vital importance; she'd never felt more strongly about anything in her life.

Once Persy had the kitten cleaned to her satisfaction, she nudged it gently with her nose, pushing the scrawny little thing toward her nipples. Lucy reached into the box and gently helped position the kitten. To her relief, it found a nipple and began sucking.

Persy half closed her eyes and began purring. Apparently there were no more kittens to be born. Or had they already been born somewhere outside? Maybe the owl had attacked Persy during the birth. If so, could any of the other kittens have survived? Lucy bit her lip, glancing at the darkness beyond her window, imagining helpless kittens needing to be rescued.

Persy's hiss brought her gaze back to the cat, who was now crouched, staring toward the window, fur ridged along her back, clearly showing that danger prowled the night.

"Lucy." The whisper coiled inside Lucy's head, as threatening as a snake ready to strike.

Instinctively her hands rose to the necklace, closing around the moonstones.

"Come to me, Lucy," the whisperer urged.

Though she mouthed a no, to her horror she felt an urge to obey, to open the window, undo the screen, climb out and join what she knew must be the vampire. She fought the impulse with all her will, but the urge grew stronger and stronger.

Lucy focused her gaze on the window. She must go; she had no choice. It was the same as when she'd been forced to climb the steps to the tower; she was helpless to resist, even though she knew the danger awaiting her. When a weight landed in her lap, she started, biting back a cry. Looking down, she saw that Persy, carrying the kitten in her mouth, had jumped from the box and was attempting to curl up on her.

Distracted from having to obey the command, she shifted position to accommodate the cat and again carefully pointed the kitten at a nipple. The warm weight of the cat made her feel secure. Then she realized that although he still summoned her, for some strange reason she was now able to resist his command.

Lucy stared down at the nursing kitten and suddenly understood that the reason wasn't so strange. Max had said all along that Persy wanted her to have this kitten and just now the tabby had very pointedly given it to her. The kitten was hers, and already the tiny, helpless animal was protecting her. Though she didn't understand how this could be possible, she accepted the truth. She and the kitten were linked, differently from the way she was linked with Max, but linked all the same. The linkage gave her the knowledge her kitten was a female.

The whispering ceased—Lucy had expected it would. The evil in the night knew she'd found a way to resist his command. Tenderly watching mother and kitten, she wasn't surprised when Max finally walked into the bedroom and said, "He's gone."

"Yes," she told him, "I know."

He gave her a searching look and she gestured toward the kitten in her lap. As he glanced at the cats, then back at her, a smile spread slowly over his face, dispelling his grimness.

"So Persy managed to save the right one," he said.

"Then there *were* other kittens?"

"I found two. Dead, sad to say. I'll bury them under the magnolia tomorrow."

Lucy sighed, then reached to touch her kitten's tiny head with the tip of her forefinger. "You can see she's black and white. I think she must be Roger's daughter."

"Roger's a tom, I take it."

"He belongs to the Pennyworths and is the neighborhood cat-fight champion."

Persy opened her eyes and gave Lucy a supercilious stare, as if to confirm that nothing less than a champion would suit her as a mate.

Max eased onto the bed. "I sensed the vampire somewhere near the cottage and I tried to get a fix on him. I almost had him pinpointed, when he vanished from my range. He called you, didn't he?"

Lucy nodded. "Because of the kitten I'm immune now."

"I hope so. But he's still in the area. We don't dare underestimate what he's capable of."

Recalling how irresistible his summons had been before Persy had dropped the kitten in her lap, Lucy grimaced. How well she knew he was dangerous. The terrible vision she'd had of Max and the vampire in the tower nibbled at the edge of her awareness, but she thrust it firmly away.

"I don't think Persy's wounds are serious," she said.

"Neither do I," Max said, "but if you'll hold the kitten so she knows it's safe, I'll see if she'll let me clean them and take a good look."

By the time he'd finished, Lucy had replaced the soiled-and-bloody sheet in the box with old, soft towels. Persy settled inside with the kitten, apparently content to have the box on the floor next to Lucy's bed.

Sitting propped against the headboard, Lucy watched while Max, obviously far from content, paced from one end of the bedroom to the other. "If only I could foresee what the vampire might be planning," he muttered. "This vision of yours—"

"Wouldn't be any help," she said hastily, clutching at the moonstones she still wore around her neck. "I saw we were in the tower with him, but there was no clue as to how we got there. Please don't ask me any more about it."

He stopped pacing and gave her a level look. "Or about Cassidy?"

"Luke has nothing to do with the vampire."

"Or with you?"

She stared at him. "You sound jealous."

"Who, me?" he asked indignantly.

She shrugged.

After a moment, he shook his head ruefully. "You because of Mina, me because of Cassidy. We should both know better. Bonded pairs have no reason to be jealous. But at least I explained about Mina."

She shot him an exasperated look. "Luke was part of a vision I had before I met you, a vision I discussed with him. And that's my final word on the subject."

Max stood by the dresser, apparently in deep thought. The room grew so quiet she could hear Persy purring.

At last he said, "I wish—" and then paused.

When he didn't go on, she said, knowing what he meant, "I wish, too."

And she did. Though there could be no other man for her but Max, ever, she wished they'd met differently. She wished they'd had the chance to have a long, dreamy, romantic courtship before plunging into the depths of a passion unlike anything she'd ever expected to experience. Most of all she wished she'd never had the vision of the tower.

I won't let him die, she vowed. I'll find a way to prove that horrible vision false.

Max crossed to the bed and sprawled on his side, propped himself on one elbow and looked at her. "I didn't want this to happen," he said. "You and me, I mean."

"So you've been telling me since the moment we met."

"Affairs between aberrants can be devastating. Even a partial bonding is hell to break."

"Are you speaking from experience?" she asked.

"Bitter experience. Something I never want to go through again. And I sure as hell don't want you to."

Uncertain what he was leading up to, she said, "Is it imperative? That we try break the bond, I mean. What if we leave things as they are?"

"It won't work," he said. "Not with the way I am."

Lucy pulled herself up straighter. "In other words, you're trying to tell me you want out."

"Damn it, no! It's too late. There's no way out this time."

His exasperation with the way things were annoyed her. "I didn't ask for any bonding," she said coolly.

"No one *asks* for bonding, especially permanent bonding—it either happens or it doesn't. And once you're sucked into a permanent bond—zap, that's it. You're stuck for life."

Sucked into. As if she'd done it on purpose! Lucy's annoyance flared into outright anger. "I refuse to believe I'm stuck with you for life. Or that you're stuck with me, which you seem to resent intensely. As far as I'm concerned, as soon as the vampire is caught, you can shake the dust of Clover off your heels for all time."

Max groaned, flipped over onto his stomach and stared down into Persy's box. "The woman doesn't understand," he muttered. "She doesn't have a clue."

"I understand this much," Lucy said tartly. "We may have to stay together for safety, but you can damn well sleep outside the covers tonight."

"Like I said," Max told Persy, "she really doesn't understand."

Lucy carried her anger with her as she got ready for bed and it tainted her thoughts after she slid under the sheet and tried to sleep. She was all too conscious of Max lying next to her in the bed. He might be on top of the sheet, but a thin piece of cotton wasn't much of a barrier.

To divert her mind from dwelling on him, she began to make a mental list of what she had to do tomorrow. Call Polly to let her know Persy and her one kitten were safe. Also thank Polly for the chicken. Work the afternoon shift at the library. Shop for groceries.

"Don't forget to buy coffee," Max muttered.

"Are you reading my mind?" she demanded, shocked.

"Can't do that. Just reminding you. I'm not a tea drinker."

Lucy remained upset about the coincidence until she finally fell into an uneasy sleep. She roused once when Max turned onto his side and put his arm around her. She poked him with her elbow and he grunted, mumbling something unintelligible. She poked him again and this time he took his arm away and turned his back to her. She also turned her back so she was facing the bedside stand, where the moonstones gleamed faintly in the darkness. As she stared at them she imagined she heard her grandmother's voice saying softly, "Go to sleep, child."

Reassured, she did.

She walked along a stretch of sand with the ocean to her right. I shouldn't be walking north, she thought, remembering how the old Cherokee woman who'd been her grandmother's friend had once said north was the direction of trouble and sorrow. But she didn't stop. The evening was warm, the sea breeze cool, the sand soft under her bare feet.

A blue haze hung over the water, the most beautiful blue she'd ever seen, though the absence of sound bothered her—no gulls mewed; the waves made no noise as they lapped the shore. Other than the sea grass

*waving gently in the breeze, not a living thing stirred
except for her.*

*She breathed deeply of the ocean-scented air and
frowned. Mixed with the bracing salt-iodine odor she
smelled death and decay. She stopped, aware she must
turn before it was too late, must reverse her path, must
head south in the direction of hope and promise.*

*Instead, she stood motionless, staring at the heav-
ing ocean waters tinted blue by the ever-thickening
haze. Suddenly a woman's figure materialized in the
haze, a woman made of mist, who drifted toward
shore without touching the water. She tried to move,
aware she stood in the mist woman's path, but she was
frozen in place.*

*Closer and closer came the hazy figure, until she felt
the chill kiss of the mist as it closed around her, choking her, blinding her. When at last the mist dispersed,
darkness had fallen and she and the mist woman were
one.*

*Though she had no mirror, she knew she'd changed.
No longer was her hair short, dark and curly; it hung
to her shoulders in auburn waves and she had brown
eyes, not hazel. She wore a short red dress that clung
to her curves, far more ample curves than she'd ever
possessed. Yet she was still herself—or was she?*

*Uncertain, she tried to turn toward the south, but
found herself slowly walking north once more, in
darkness lighted by the red moon climbing the night
sky—her brother would call it a hunter's moon. But
she was not a hunter. From far off came the faint howl
of a dog and she understood then that she was the prey
of the hunter who prowled the night with his black
dog.*

Once she'd known the dog's name as well as who the hunter was, but along with the change in her appearance had come a mental blurring. She was and was not herself; she'd been transformed into another. Who was this well-endowed woman in red with auburn hair and brown eyes?

The dog howled again, closer now, infinitely menacing. There was no place to run except northward, into the tainted air, into the place of death and decay. Part of her understood she must stay where she was and face the hunter, but the woman she'd become, terrorized by the menace hunting her, began to run.

As she ran, a name surfaced. "Mina!" she screamed. "Mina, Mina, Mina—no!"

Her shoulders were gripped by strong hands that shook her. Struggling to free herself, she opened her eyes and, though unable to see him clearly in the darkness, immediately knew it was Max who held her.

"Max!" she cried, collapsing into his embrace.

"Nightmare?" he murmured.

"I dreamed I was Mina," she said. "And I—she—we were being hunted."

"By the vampire?" he asked.

"I think so." The oddity of the dream struck her and she pulled away from Max. "How strange to dream about her."

"Maybe you were trying to get rid of poor Mina." Amusement threaded his words.

"Then why was I still a part of her, so whatever hunted us was after me, too?" She glanced at the bedside stand, where she knew the necklace rested. "The last thing I remember before the dream began is looking at the glow of the moonstones."

After a moment, he said, "I don't see any glow."

Lucy realized she didn't, either, not now, so she reached to the stand and groped around until she felt the familiar shape of the gems under her hand. "They're not glowing now, but the necklace is still there," she told him.

"Maybe you dreamed the glow."

"I think I was still awake, because I'd just turned over after poking you with my elbow."

He eased an arm around her shoulders. "Why would you poke me?"

She lifted his arm from her shoulders. "Because you were trying to do this very same thing—although you were asleep then."

"At least I didn't try to do this."

Before she knew what he intended, his mouth slanted over hers. His kiss evoked an instant response, one she found impossible to deny. After a long moment she found the will to ease away far enough to whisper against his lips, "Unfair."

"Why? I know you want what I want—I can feel your need almost as intensely as I can my own." Without waiting for her to answer in words, he deepened the kiss, wrapping his arms around her.

Before she gave herself up to the desire blazing inside her, she admitted the truth of what he'd said. How could she not, when in the same way he sensed her need, she could sense his—the bond worked both ways.

His hand slid under her shirt and she sighed in pleasure as his fingers caressed her skin. Was it the bond that told him exactly how and where to touch her? If so, she should be able to sense what he wanted *her* to do....

He drew in his breath as she began to caress him and the feel of his delighted pleasure increased her own.

"Unfair," he said hoarsely. "You're learning too much about me."

"Nothing's unfair between us," she murmured. "You said so yourself."

As she returned to her intimate and fascinated exploration of his body, she caught a glint of light from the corner of her eye. Though bemused almost past caring about anything but making love to Max, she turned her head to look. The moonstones were glowing.

An instant later, Max abruptly pulled away from her and cursed. "The bastard's homed in on us."

She heard Persy's low growl, then she felt the invasion, too, an alien presence contaminating the wonder between them. She snatched up the necklace, holding the moonstones to her breast.

Go away! she cried soundlessly. *Get out!*

The evil presence vanished as suddenly as it had come.

"You got rid of him," Max said, relief in his voice. "I couldn't because it's you he's connected to through that damn bridal necklace he gave you. He got to me because of the bonding uniting us when we make love."

"He really is gone, then?"

"From us, yes. But I can sense him at the edge of my range, so he's on the prowl, not too far off."

She edged closer to Max. "In the yard?"

"No, farther than that. In fact, my sense of him is fading, so he's heading away from here." Max covered her hand with his. "Damn him! What's between us is ours."

"That's true, but his interference means we don't dare make love. I couldn't bear it if this happened to us again."

Max swore under his breath, his jaw clenching. "He's gotten stronger. That means he's taken a victim to draw energy from."

Lucy, shuddering to think of what must be happening to anyone within the vampire's power, tightened her grip on the necklace. Glancing at the moonstones, she noticed they were no longer glowing as they had been just before Max had felt the vampire's presence.

"Max," she said, "the moonstones have more power than we thought. I believe they warn of danger." She went on to tell him what she'd observed, adding, "And I was holding them when I ordered him to leave."

"You may be right. If so, that's a real plus." He flicked on the bedside lamp and got to his feet. "I won't sleep again tonight."

"Neither will I." Lucy rose, too. "I'll make some tea."

"I suppose tea's better than nothing," he said, doubt tinging his voice.

"I think there's still at least one leg left of Polly's fried chicken—and it's all yours. I'm going to make myself some toast."

After Persy appeared with the kitten in her mouth, Max carried the box to the kitchen and persuaded the cat to settle inside again. "Looks as though you'll have to move the box from room to room with you," he told Lucy.

Touched by Persy's insistence on being close to her, Lucy nodded. "I don't mind."

Max ate the chicken leg plus three pieces of toast with homemade blackberry jam. "It's the only way I can get the tea down," he said. "We're going to be the diner's first customers in the morning. Peg makes a mean cup of coffee, and I sure need one. On the way home I intend to buy you a very large supply of coffee."

"What do we do with Persy?" Lucy asked.

"I suggest closing her, box, kitten and all, in your little pantry until we come back. Otherwise she may decide to hide her baby somewhere in the cottage the way mother cats often do and we'll have a devil of a time finding the kitten."

As early as they got to Peg's Diner, though, they weren't the first. Five others had beaten them there. When Peg brought their coffee, she glanced at Max, then leaned closer to Lucy and said, "You heard the news?"

"What news?" Lucy asked, certain Peg meant something local. National and international events didn't qualify.

"About Mina, I mean," Peg said, darting another look at Max.

Mina. Dread closed Lucy's throat. Had her dream been a warning?

"You mean Mina Martin?" Max asked Peg.

Lucy sensed the effort it took for him to keep his tone casual.

"She's missing," Peg said. "Around midnight some kids out gigging frogs found her car abandoned down by Honeycutt Creek, over near the old oyster crushing plant. No sign of her at all."

The vampire, Lucy thought in horror. Max suspected he'd found a victim. Oh, God, poor Mina. She clenched her coffee cup.

"I felt sure you'd have heard something about it from your brother," Peg added.

"Ford never talks to me about his work," Lucy said automatically, repeating what she'd said so many times over the years. It was the absolute truth.

Peg shifted her gaze to Max. "I guess he didn't tell you, either," she said.

Max shook his head.

"Must make you feel kind of funny, you having taken Mina out and all," Peg said.

"Naturally I'm concerned for her safety," Max said, his grim expression belying the calmness of his voice.

Evidently deciding she wasn't likely to get anything more from the two of them, Peg bustled off.

"Drink your coffee, Lucy," Max ordered, speaking in a low tone. "I'm as eager to get out of here as you are, but appearances count. If we go dashing off, leaving two full cups of coffee, Peg will suspect more than she does already, and this diner is a hotbed of gossip."

Aware he was right, Lucy did her best to obey, but found it hard to swallow. "What is it you think Peg suspects?" she asked, keeping her voice down.

"Me. And she won't be the only one who does. I'm the stranger in town, remember."

She stared at him. "But you couldn't possibly have had anything to do with—"

"Only you know that for sure. Could you swear to your brother that I was with you every minute? Think about it. I wasn't, you know. The vampire's counting on me being questioned and maybe being put under surveillance, so my movements will be restricted. That's why he picked Mina. Once again the bastard's a step ahead of me."

CHAPTER TWELVE

"What can we do about Mina?" Lucy asked as they drove back to the cottage. "I can't bear to think of what might have happened to her."

"I suspect she's still alive," Max said. "He means to use her for bait as well as feed on her energy. I'm a nuisance to the vampire. He intends to finish me off one way or another so nothing stands between him and you. I'm responsible for involving Mina, so he knows I'll come after her. He's turned the tables on me—Mina's still the lure, but now I'm the fish to be netted."

"You can't go anywhere if Ford decides you may be guilty of abducting Mina and puts you in jail," Lucy commented, almost hoping that would happen so Max would be safe. She was immediately ashamed of the thought. Max was Mina's only chance to survive.

"I doubt it will come to that—your brother's no fool."

Lucy nodded agreement and said nothing more. When they arrived home, she put coffee on to brew before checking on Persy and her kitten, finding them both still in the box in the pantry. Leaving the pantry door open, she began unpacking the groceries. Max, she knew, was on the phone.

She had the coffee poured and waiting by the time Max came into the kitchen.

"I told Polly we had Persy and her kitten over here," he said, easing onto a chair. "I also spoke to your brother."

"What did Ford say?"

Max smiled wryly. "Since Mina's abandoned car was found, several people have come by or phoned to tell him he'd better check me out. He will, sooner or later. For now, he's looking for other leads. Without any suggestion on my part, he suspects Dooley may be involved and is getting a search warrant so he can investigate the Franklin mansion and grounds."

"Honeycutt Creek isn't near the mansion," she said.

"Ford is as aware of that as you are. But he didn't trust Dooley from the first—your brother has a feel for wrongness. Besides his instinctive mistrust of Dooley, it seems one of the old men who hang out near the library told him that he'd known 'them redheaded Dooleys from way, way back' and he had his doubts that the so-called nephew who claimed Letitia Franklin's estate could possibly be a Dooley."

"Ford never told me that."

"He said you were hell-bent on marrying Dooley, and he had no proof there was anything wrong with the man. If you remember, he did ask you to wait for a while."

Lucy sighed. "I should have listened. I guess part of the problem was I'd grown tired of always taking my brother's advice."

"You were also under the vampire's influence—don't discount how powerful that was."

Lucy set down her coffee mug. How well she knew and feared that power! But she refused to let that stop her from trying to help Mina escape the vampire's coils.

"I've made up my mind I'm going with you on your search for Mina," she said.

Max frowned at her. "Unmake it. You're not going. I'll have enough on my hands without worrying about you."

"He can't influence me now that I'm bound to the kitten."

Max shook his head. "The kitten's a newborn and fragile. If you're with her and Persy she can use her mother's strength and not be harmed, but if you were at a distance and needing help, the stress of the bond might kill her."

Lucy stared at him, horrified. Was he telling her the truth? "Could I really kill Medea by calling on her for help?" she blurted.

"So you've given her a witch's name. Good. And yes, until she's fully grown she won't be able to offer protection without endangering herself."

Lucy, who hadn't even realized she'd named the kitten, mulled over his words.

"That's why you can't come with me," he said. "You're safe here, so I won't have to worry about the vampire reaching you while I'm gone. But if you weren't with Persy and Medea, he might be able to."

Later, Lucy watched uneasily as Max pulled his black case from under her bed and prepared to leave with it. She didn't understand how he used the contents of the case, but she feared that no matter how powerful the ingredients were, the vampire could overcome them.

Though she didn't doubt Max's courage or his abilities as an aberrant, the vampire was still on the loose and she wondered if such an evil creature could ever be bested or caged.

Tucked away in the back of her mind was the memory of her appalling vision in the mansion's tower. In that vision the vampire had been the victor. On the other hand, she'd been with Max. Did that mean he was safe for the time being?

"Are you going to the mansion?" she asked.

"Ford promised to let me know what he found there, if anything. I can't imagine the vampire being careless enough to take Mina to the mansion, so I doubt your brother will turn up much."

"You didn't answer my question."

He raised his quirked eyebrow higher. "You Maguires can be persistent. I'll certainly drive by to see if I sense the vampire's presence. That's the best answer I can give at the moment."

He started for the bedroom door, but she blocked his path. "Max . . ." Her voice trailed off as she discovered she was unable to say the words rising from her heart—*I love you.* "Come back," she said finally.

He gazed down at her, his eyes unreadable. "I'll try," he said. "For the first time in years I have something to come back to." He brushed his lips over hers, gently eased her aside and strode toward the front door.

She hurried after him, standing in the open doorway to watch him leave. Only after his car had vanished from her view did she close and then lock the door.

I'll try. Unsatisfactory words, but, given the formidable opponent he faced, realistic ones, words she had to live with.

Max drove first to Honeycutt Creek because he had a hunch the vampire might have purposefully left some clue that only he would recognize, a clue that would leave him certain Mina was in the vampire's power.

Mina's car had been towed from the site, but fragments of police yellow tape still remained to show where it had been found. Max parked and slid from his car, standing in the bright morning, the sun warm on his shoulders. A mockingbird sang from somewhere on the other side of the creek, jumbling several bird songs to create its own original melody.

The scent of honeysuckle sweetened the dampness of the air as he walked from the road and stepped underneath trees tangled with wild grapevine. Something plopped into the water as he approached—probably one of the frogs the boys who found the abandoned car had been hoping to gig.

Evil didn't belong in this peaceful setting. Nor should evil be stalking the streets of Clover, disturbing the town's tranquillity. Shuck should never have been turned loose here; the devil dog belonged in hell. And the vampire? A creature who belonged nowhere, an abomination that shouldn't be allowed to live.

Max paced slowly along the creek bank, his gaze searching for anything that seemed out of place. He was about ready to turn back, when he spotted a glint of gold within the twisting tendrils of a grapevine. He zeroed in on a delicate gold chain, probed it psychically to make certain no trap had been set and finally reached to free the chain from the coils of the vine.

He felt a tingle when he touched it, not of evil but of familiarity. Not until his find was in his hand, though, did he see the tiny gold *O* suspended from the chain. A shock of recognition arrowed through him. *Olivia!* He held his dead sister's chain.

As his hand closed around the chain, a deadly fury gripped Max. The bastard mocked him, did he?

Back in the car, Max took deep, shuddering breaths, letting the air out slowly, striving to regain his calm. Anger fogged the mind and only a fool would set off on any quest without a clear mind. He needed every sense honed and ready to face his wily and dangerous foe.

Highgate Road was his next objective. As he neared the gates of the Franklin mansion, he saw the sheriff's cruiser between them, pulling onto the road, so he honked, waved, drove onto the shoulder and parked. A few moments later, Ford eased in behind him. They both got out.

"Any sign of Dooley?" Max asked.

Ford shook his head. "We went through the grounds, then the house room by room. He's not there. Doesn't appear he's been around the place recently, either."

"How about the tower room?"

"Nothing," Ford said. "Great view from up there, though, with all those floor-to-ceiling windows."

The cruiser radio crackled into life. Ford listened, made a clipped response and turned back to Max. "Some idiot robbed one of our branch banks at noon yesterday. The camera got a good shot of him and now it looks like we've IDed him. I'll talk to you later."

"Any objection if I drive onto the estate grounds?"

Ford shrugged. "Who's to care?" He got back into the car, made a U-turn and roared off.

Max didn't enter the estate through the gates. Instead he drove along the road past the mansion, his special sense alert for any indication of the vampire. He'd almost come to the end of the grounds, when he felt the first intimation that the vampire was within his psychic range.

Recalling the gas station pay phone Ford had said Lucy's call had come from, Max kept on toward the first crossroads, his feeling that the vampire was in the vicinity growing stronger and stronger.

When he reached the crossroads, he pulled into the combination convenience store and station and went inside to buy a soft drink. Glancing casually around, he spotted a pay phone.

As he paid for the soda, he said to the middle-aged woman clerk, "Any places to stay nearby? Like cabins or maybe a campground?"

"No campgrounds hereabouts," she said. "You got to go closer to the ocean for that."

"Cabins?" he repeated.

She looked him over. "Well, yeah, a couple, but none *you'd* want to stay in."

"Depends on how cheap they are."

"They're down a dirt road about half a mile north of here. The sign says Lapham's, but it's pretty faded. Take a look if you want, but don't say I didn't warn you what you'd get."

"Thanks."

Max ambled away from the store, careful to show no haste, got into his car and pulled away in an equally relaxed fashion. By the time he spotted the faded sign—only the *L* and the *p* were clear enough to read—his sense of the vampire was so strong that the psychic vibrations thrummed through him.

Easy does it, he warned himself as he turned onto the dirt road. Now that you're bonded with Lucy, he can sense you, too.

The road was little more than a single-lane rutted trail with brush and saplings pushing close to either side. Max stopped the car and left it blocking the road. Instead of choosing to walk along the road toward the cabins, he slipped into the sparse woods and made his way cautiously through the brushy growth.

When he spotted the peeling paint and sagging roofs of the cluster of five cabins Max paused, grimacing as he visualized the sordid interiors. Three of the cabins seemed to be occupied, one obviously the owner's or manager's because it bore a sign reading Office. Otherwise that cabin was in the same run-down condition as the others.

A van with a Texas license plate was parked beside the cabin closest to the office. The cabin at the far end of the cluster had a nondescript pickup next to it with a battered South Carolina plate. All Max's instincts told him the vampire was very close. In one of the cabins?

From the office came the faint beat of a boom box playing country music, but otherwise he could detect no sounds. There should at least be birds calling. He glanced all around, suspecting a trap, but detected nothing other than the faint odor of onions cooking.

Tempted to circle toward the cabin at the far end of the clearing, Max shook his head. The vampire must be waiting for him to make a move. Why? What would happen when he did? Then again, he could be wrong. Maybe the bastard was a step ahead of him once more and, figuring he'd be too suspicious to be lured into rash action, had counted on Max's cautiousness. He could be doing exactly what the vampire wanted.

Gripped by frustration, Max swore under his breath. Damned if he did and damned if he didn't—was that it? Possibly the vampire, though he may have been staying here, wasn't in any of the cabins at the moment but hiding in the woods, his trap already set. In that case, it was likely, Max told himself grimly, that he'd already walked into the damn trap, whatever it was.

A distant siren caught his attention. Cop's car, he decided after listening closely. Coming closer. A nasty possibility occurred to him. Abandoning any attempt to be quiet, he whirled around and raced back toward his car. As he ran, he grew conscious that his perception of the vampire was fading.

He pounded up to his car and looked inside. Bloody hell! The bastard had framed him. Mina lay sprawled naked on his back seat. Not dead—he sensed a flicker of life—but minutes away from death. The siren shrieked, very near now.

Without hesitation, Max jerked open the door, reached in, lifted Mina over his shoulder, kicked the door shut and trotted into the woods with her. Reaching a fairly thick growth of small pines, he eased her to the ground, dropped down beside her, yanked off his shirt and gathered her into his arms. Her only chance was if he was able to transfer enough of his energy to her to allow her to survive until the medics could help her. Since he wasn't bonded to Mina, he couldn't do it alone—he needed Lucy.

Pressing Mina's cold body against his, he closed his eyes and, while picturing Lucy, sent a psychic message, unsure whether she'd receive it or not.

Help me. Activate the bond. Join with me. Help me.

For long moments, nothing happened. Mina's life was flickering like a candle flame about to gutter out, when a surge of energy flooded through him, the excess seeping through his skin into Mina, renewing her. When at last he released her, though she was still unconscious, she'd revived enough to moan.

The siren peaked to a crescendo and stopped abruptly. Max quickly pulled on his shirt. As he lifted Mina into his arms he became aware how much the energy drain had weakened him. He carried her into a small clearing, saw the flashing red lights through the thin cover of brush, laid her down, nodded in satisfaction when she moaned again and trotted off through the woods away from the red lights and from his car.

He no longer sensed the vampire, but he thought he knew where the bastard had gone, and he headed in the same direction—toward the Franklin mansion. The energy loss told on him and his pace soon slowed to a tired walk.

The vampire had almost put him out of action. If the authorities had found Mina dead in his car he'd be in deep trouble. And he still was in a mess. Once they spotted her—and they would soon enough, guided by her moans—they'd continue to search for him until Mina regained consciousness sometime later, in the hospital. Only when she could talk and tell them what had happened to her would he be off the hook. Considering the trauma she'd suffered, though, she might not be rational for a day or two.

He scowled as he slogged wearily on. The vampire must have picked up a cellular phone somewhere to be able to call 911 so easily once he was certain Max had stepped into his trap. It had been a clever plan that had come within a breath—Mina's breath—of succeeding.

"You haven't won yet, Vampire," Max muttered. "I'm still free and I'm on your trail. Sooner or later we'll meet face-to-face. And then—"

Then? Max knew it would be a struggle to the death. Because of his own energy deficit, he could only hope the energy stolen from Mina hadn't been enough for the vampire to regain his full power.

No confrontation would take place unless he managed to reach the Franklin estate—on foot—without being picked up by the cops. Then he had to get into the house, avoiding traps. He stumbled, fell to one knee and paused a few minutes before getting up. Damn, he was weak.

He tried to go on, but when he began to stagger he realized he'd never make it unless he stopped to rest to give his energy level time to rebuild.

Max's hand closed around Olivia's gold chain, carried in his pocket. He'd win. He had to. To avenge his sister. But even more important, to save the woman who meant more to him than his life. To save Lucy.

* * *

Lucy lay on her stomach on her bed, peering into Persy's box, regarding Medea anxiously. The kitten nursed vigorously enough, but she was so very tiny and helpless. Max's unexpected call for help hadn't seemed to affect either mother or daughter, which was a relief.

Lucy felt drained, as though she'd run miles and miles after a hard day's work. His demand had startled her, but she'd been just as surprised to discover she knew how to respond. She turned over onto her back, reached for the moonstones and ran the necklace through her fingers as she relived the strange sensation of willingly offering an intangible part of herself to Max.

She hoped what she'd done *had* helped him. If only she knew where he was and what was happening. When her brother had finally returned her call a few minutes ago, he'd been terse and uncommunicative— as though he had something to hide. The only real information Ford had given her was that the search of the Franklin mansion and grounds had been negative.

Maybe she ought to call her brother back and tell him she believed he was concealing something from her and if it concerned Max, she had a right to know. Yes, that's what she'd do. Right after she rested a bit. She couldn't ever remember feeling quite so tired....

The darkness was illuminated by seven softly glowing globes that showed her a figure standing at the foot of her bed. Her grandmother.

"The time has come," Grandma said.

What time? Lucy wondered.

As if she'd spoken aloud, her grandmother answered.

"The time to leave all that is safe and venture into the unknown. The time to reach within yourself and discover what you are. The time to destroy evil so you may gain love."

"I don't understand," Lucy said.

"Trust in yourself. You will understand as you need to. Heed me, blood of my blood—*it is time!*"

Lucy awoke with her grandmother's words ringing in her ears. For a few moments she wasn't sure whether she was in or out of a dream because, though it had been afternoon when she'd lain down on the bed, darkness surrounded her except for a soft glow.

The moonstones! The necklace lay across her breasts, the gems gleaming softly.

Lucy sat up, and impelled by the knowledge she must, she put on the necklace, struggling, as usual, with the clasp. Glancing at the green numerals of the clock, she saw it was not quite eight. Wasn't it uncommonly dark for this time of the evening?

A far-off rumble of thunder told her why. It was fixing to storm.

Once she came fully awake, she realized the moonstones, now around her neck, were still glowing, something they didn't do except as a warning. Something was wrong.

Lucy flicked on the bedside lamp and leaned across the bed to look at the cats. Persy slitted her eyes and yawned; Medea squirmed closer to her mother and began to nurse. Since Persy wasn't upset, the warning couldn't be of nearby danger.

Max! The moonstones must be glowing because he was in trouble and needed her help. Lucy leaped to her feet and slid on her sandals. She still wore the jeans and T-shirt she'd had on all day, so she was ready to go. But go where? She didn't have any idea where Max was.

Her hands rose to touch the glowing gems, as she hoped for a vision that would lead her to Max. As soon as she felt the warmth of the moonstones under her fingers, the terrible realization came to her that she'd already had the vision, a vision that had shown her Max in the tower of the Franklin mansion. With the vampire.

Lucy tried unsuccessfully to swallow the metallic taste of fear that rose to her tongue. The vision had also shown her in the tower. Which meant she must go there. But how could she force herself to go to the place she dreaded more than anywhere else in the world?

A bolt of lightning flashed, thunder rolled, there was a booming crash outside and her bedroom lamp went out. The electricity had been cut off. Would it be off in the tower, too?

The thought of opening the front door of the mansion and entering in the dark terrified her. Taking a deep breath, she tried to gather her courage. Don't merely react—use your reason, she admonished herself.

Max needed her. Therefore, afraid or not, she was going to him. Flashlights dispelled darkness; she owned flashlights. If she didn't think about the tower until she had to face climbing the stairs, she could control her fright.

A calming thought made her sigh in relief. She didn't need to go alone, she could call her brother and ask him to go with her. Hurrying to the phone, she put it to her ear. No dial tone. She tried punching in numbers, but nothing happened. The phone was dead.

I'll stop by his house, she decided.

Wind and rain impeded her dash to her car. She'd no sooner pulled into the street than her headlights shone on a huge branch that lay across the road, wires tangled around it. She reversed, turned and took a detour. Before she reached Ford's, a sheriff's car shot past her, siren howling, red lights revolving, and streaked out of sight.

Her heart sank. Though Ford might not have been in that particular car, she knew he'd be in another, because he took his job seriously. Most likely there were other downed limbs, and since she saw no lights in any of the houses she passed, that probably meant the electricity was out all over the town.

So she was on her own.

No, not really. If her vision held true, Max would be at the mansion, so she'd be with Max. In the tower room. Lucy fought to keep from reliving the entire vision. He won't die, she vowed. Grandma told me it was time for me to step into the unknown and gain love. Her words must mean there's a way to save Max, if only I can discover what that way is.

The wind battered her small car, making her grip the wheel tensely in order to stay on the road. Rain slashed across the windshield in such a flood that the wipers were practically useless. She'd been right about limbs down; she skirted one after another, seeing them barely in time to avoid smashing into them.

When she reached the street that led to Highgate Road, she saw a battery of lights ahead, some flashing red, and slowed to a crawl. As she neared she saw an entire tree—a pine—had fallen across the street, blocking it completely.

Damn! The only other other way to get to Highgate Road would lead her a couple of miles out of the way. In this storm that would take time she couldn't spare. Holding her breath, Lucy, determinedly ignoring the signals to stop, swung her car to the left, into a driveway, bumped across the lawns of two houses, through a hedge, and exited from another drive into the street beyond the fallen tree.

Immediately after she turned onto Highgate Road, she splashed through water covering her hubcaps, the water pouring across the road with such velocity she had to fight to keep the car from being swept along with it. Lightning illuminated her surroundings with an eerie green glow and thunder crashed so violently she winced at each jolt.

A storm from hell, she thought, then couldn't keep from wondering if the vampire had somehow conjured it up. No, she told herself, he may be powerful but he's not *all*-powerful. And since he's not, he can be beaten.

Her first meeting with him flashed across her mind as forcefully as the lightning bolts zigzagging around her. She once again turned and saw Bela Lugosi's Dracula staring at her, an image that vanished and became Joe Dooley's handsome face.

Except he wasn't Joe Dooley. Joseph R. Dooley was dead, murdered. And he wasn't Bela Lugosi's movie Dracula, either. He was a real vampire. Not the mythic kind with fangs who sucked blood from victims' throats, but a vampire nonetheless. He was a creature who drained life from others by stealing their life force—not blood, but what some might call the spirit. What Max called energy.

Beneath the vampire's handsome face dwelled a monster. And to think she'd almost married him!

Was poor Mina still alive? Lucy bit her lip. Much as she pitied Mina, Max was who she really feared for. What was happening in that dreadful tower?

CHAPTER THIRTEEN

Because of his bone-deep fatigue, the journey to the Franklin estate took on the aspect of a nightmare to Max. As in a dream, where no matter how many obstacles the dreamer overcomes he never attains his goal, so Max's desperate struggle to keep moving seemed to bring him no closer to the mansion.

He rested at increasingly shorter intervals, only to find himself as exhausted when he rose as when he'd sat down. During the last rest, at the far reaches of the estate grounds, he fell into a profound sleep under a giant sweet gum. A warning rumble of thunder roused him to darkness and the realization he'd slept far too long.

Hours had passed, wasted hours. Yet as he forced himself to his feet, he decided the time hadn't been completely wasted. He couldn't deny the sleep had revived him and renewed his strength, making him feel more like himself, though he was by no means fully recovered.

His special sense told him the vampire was still in the vicinity. Did the bastard sense him, as well? Considering how low his energy had been, Max thought, it was possible the vampire hadn't been able to detect him. But he couldn't count on it. It could prove fatal to assume anything where that monster was concerned.

Since the vampire hadn't seized the chance to escape, possibly he wasn't aware of Max or, more likely, he was waiting for Max to come to him. Max controlled his impulse to plunge ahead in a frantic dash for the mansion—no use wasting his still-not-up-to-par strength in either case. Instead he conserved his energy by striding through the gloom, making no effort to conceal himself.

If the cops were searching for him, the darkness and the dense landscaping of the grounds would prevent him from being seen from the road. Or from the house, though he doubted they were at the mansion. But he strongly suspected the vampire was there, and with his energy level increased, the vampire didn't need to see him, because the bastard would be able to sense his approach in the same way that the closer he came to the mansion, the stronger became the psychic vibrations that warned him of the vampire's presence.

No lights shone from any of the windows, but he hadn't expected any. The vampire wasn't such a fool as to advertise his whereabouts. Lightning streaked across the sky and the following rumble of thunder came quickly, warning Max the storm had almost reached the estate. He increased his pace, feeling the first drops of rain on his face.

When he reached the outbuilding nearest the house, a potting shed attached to a small greenhouse, a creaking noise made him pause. A lightning flash showed him the door to the shed was open. Rain began to sluice down. Feeling no hint of a psychic trap, Max decided the police search earlier might account for the open door and so he risked taking temporary shelter within the shed.

He was now convinced the vampire had holed up in the tower and that quite probably he'd stopped along the way to set traps. To go dashing inside the house risked stepping into one of those traps. Caution was the name of this game. In an effort to tamp down his impatience at having to go slow, he fingered the gold chain in his pocket, gradually coming to realize he possessed more than a memento of Olivia. Because her chain had been in the vampire's possession, it could be used as a weapon against him.

Removing the chain, Max held it by the attached *O*, the letter representing her name, and closed his eyes to better evoke her image. He visualized Olivia as she had been in life—laughing and vibrant—then as he'd last seen her, a pitiful horror he'd never forget as long as he lived.

Avenge your owner, he urged the chain, painstakingly threading his images of Olivia through its links. When he finished, he slipped it over his right arm and secured the chain within the rolled sleeve of the water-soaked black shirt he wore.

Lightning flashed almost constantly, with no time between the vivid bursts and the thundering roars. Violent gusts of wind plucked branches from the trees and blew the rain inside the open shed door. No matter how dangerous the storm might be, he knew the vampire was far more deadly. Armed with Olivia's chain and his own determination to put an end to the monster, Max plunged grimly into the storm, fighting the wind as he ran toward the mansion.

He found the back door unlocked and regarded it with suspicion—too convenient? Stepping out from under the portico shielding the back entrance, he

groped for and found one of the bricks used as a dec-
orative barrier between plantings alongside the house
and the lawn. Waiting for a lightning flash, he aimed
and flung the brick at an unscreened window, timing
it so the shattering of the glass was hidden by the crash
of thunder.

After using part of a fallen branch to knock the remaining glass from the old wooden frame, he hoisted
himself up and through the window. When he dropped
to the floor he landed where he'd expected, in the
butler's pantry off the kitchen.

With the irregular illumination of the lightning
guiding him, he eased warily in. There was no question in his mind that the vampire knew he'd entered
the house and was waiting in the tower, like a spider in
its web, for his next move.

Because the back door had been unlocked, Max
figured on a trap somewhere between the kitchen and
the back stairs to the second floor because that would
be the quickest way for anyone to reach the tower
stairs. Since the vampire wasn't likely to overlook the
alternative route, Max didn't rule out a second trap set
on the way from the kitchen to the main staircase in
the front entry.

Proceeding inch by careful inch, he sent psychic
probes ahead and located the expected trap embed-
ded in the door that opened onto the back stairs. It
was relatively simple to defuse. When his probing
didn't reveal anything dangerous on the steps, he
started up them. He made no attempt to be quiet,
aware the vampire had other means than sound to locate him.

Max banished everything from his mind but his goal. Never mind his water-soaked clothes; they didn't matter. With such a deadly enemy to outwit, there was no room for discomfort or for memories of Olivia or the hope that Mina had survived. Nor did he dare cling to the slightest thought of the one person who meant more to him than anyone else in the world. Lucy. At least he had the satisfaction of knowing that at this moment Lucy was safe.

He mounted the steps methodically, not making the mistake of taking anything for granted. The door at the top of the flight was closed, but he didn't detect a trap, so he opened it, not stepping into the second-floor corridor until his probe told him there was no danger.

Reaching the door leading to the tower stairs, he paused, sensing trouble ahead. His probe revealed an intricate, many-faceted trap connected to the door, one that would be a real challenge to defuse. And, unfortunately, the process used energy he could ill afford to use with the vampire still to be faced.

By the time he'd disconnected the twelve psychic threads that, if any one was broken, would trigger the trap, Max could feel the drain. He started to reach for the doorknob and held with his hand still in the air, a tingling along his spine warning him something was not right. He drew back his hand and very carefully probed what he'd thought was the defused trap. He persisted until he found a well-hidden thirteenth thread.

Finally certain the trap was completely defused, he opened the door and set his foot on the first step that led to the room at the top of the tower. The darkness was not as complete as he'd anticipated because the lightning flashing beyond the tower windows sent intermittent light down the stairs. In addition, there was a reddish glow above. Max suspected the glow had no ordinary source.

Twenty-one steps, Lucy had told him after she'd been forced to climb seven of them. As quickly as he could, he shut her out of his mind, but the number seven stuck. Stopping on the sixth step, he intensified his probe and discovered the seventh step didn't register at all psychically. Whatever had been done to it resisted identification.

When he'd exhausted every method of probing he knew without success, Max came to a decision. Though he had no intention of setting foot on that dangerous seventh step, he made up his mind he had no choice but to take the risk of stepping over it, from six to eight.

Chanting a protection spell under his breath, he started to make the step, then suddenly, without conscious thought but alert to obey any hunch, he stretched farther and landed on the ninth step instead of the eighth.

"You're improving, Ryder." The vampire's voice slithered down from the room above. "If you had the time you might even grow enough to become a worthy opponent. No doubt you won't believe me, but that was the last of the traps. You're now invited to step into my parlor."

Max mentally finished the quote. *Said the spider to the fly.* Not relaxing his caution, he probed his way up to the top and, once he got there, glanced quickly about the circular room.

In the reddish glow, whose source he couldn't discern, he saw floor-to-ceiling windows separated by wood panels, a parquet floor and no furnishings except for a narrow-and-low brass bed in the exact center of the room. On the bed was a crimson coverlet bound with gold.

The vampire stood by one of the windows, a chilling smile on his face. "You've become a nuisance, Ryder," he said. "You've inconvenienced me to the point where I can no longer ignore you. You signed your death sentence when you interfered with my marriage to Lucy Maguire. As you die, you'll learn too late that persistence is no substitute for skill."

Max refused to be goaded into a response, continuing to view the vampire warily, alert for a psychic attack. What came was not at all what he'd expected. With a sudden twist of his wrist, the vampire flung an object toward him, something that coiled, shimmering in the red glow.

Max managed to abort his instinctive impulse to bat whatever it was away from him and ducked to the side, instead, barely escaping being struck. The object clattered to the floor, slid along it and dropped to the top step. He stared down at a necklace of diamonds and sapphires—Lucy's bridal gift from the vampire. What would have happened if he'd touched the thing he had no idea.

"I compliment you on your reflexes," the vampire said.

At the same time he blasted Max with a psychic blow so powerful that some of the evil leaked past Max's protective shield, staggering him. As he struggled to recover, the vampire leaped over the bed and dived at him, knocking him backward to the floor.

Strong hands fastened around Max's throat.

After skidding along the mud-slicked drive, Lucy finally parked her car near the front door of the mansion. To her it seemed that the storm hung over the estate like a judgment, the lightning blinding, the thunder deafening. Though she ran as fast as she could from her car to the door, the slashing rain had soaked through her raincoat by the time she ducked under the entrance roof.

She had the key in the pocket of the coat, but tried the doorknob first and discovered the door was unlocked. Hesitantly she pushed it open, flicking on her flashlight before entering. As she passed through the open door she felt a tugging, as though something were trying to hold her back. When the moonstones on her necklace began to glow brightly, the sensation disappeared. Had she passed through a trap?

Once inside, she shut the door and flashed the light around the entry. At the foot of the staircase, two red circles glowed. Hair rose on her nape. What were they? As she focused the light on the the circles, they began to move toward her, a darkness coalescing around them to form a black shape. When she saw the gleam of sharp white teeth below what she realized belatedly were red eyes, she gasped and cringed against the door, frozen in terror.

Shuck!

She was trapped. This time she couldn't possibly escape him.

As she braced herself for his attack, a conviction arrowed into her mind. Shuck shouldn't be here; Max had told her she'd banished him once and for all during her out-of-the-body experience. But this time she was in her body. Did that make a difference?

Taking a deep breath, she forced one shaking hand to focus the flashlight directly on Shuck, while with her other hand she gripped the moonstones. Feeling their warmth against her skin gave her courage. She'd faced this devil dog before and won.

In her mind, she pictured the rays of the flashlight as borrowing the glow of the moonstones, deadly to Shuck. Reaching into her memory, she relived the way he'd once dissolved as if the glow of the gems had been the sun's rays dispersing a noxious fog.

"Begone!" she cried, the word rising to her tongue from the time before.

She blinked in relieved disbelief when he suddenly vanished as though he'd never been more than a figment of her imagination. Recalling how Max had spoken of traps, she decided maybe that's what Shuck had been—a psychic trap set by the vampire.

Did that mean the vampire had known she'd be coming to the mansion? Lucy controlled a shudder. What *was* she doing here? She didn't know for certain Max was in the tower. All she had to go on was her feeling that's where he was, her feeling and the terrible vision she'd had of him wrestling with the vampire in the tower.

Was that enough? At this very moment, perhaps Max was unlocking the door to the cottage and going inside, expecting to find her there. Instead she stood alone in the entry hall of the Franklin mansion. Was the vampire in the tower waiting for her? Had he somehow called her here?

As she hesitated at the foot of the main staircase, lightning illuminated the hall with a ghastly brilliance and a particularly vicious clap of thunder rattled the windows, unnerving her. What should she do? Go on or turn back? Where was Max?

If she turned back, fought her way home through the storm and found Max was not at the cottage, what would she do then? Luke Cassidy's confession flashed into her mind. His words had confirmed the truth of the vision she'd had of him. All her visions had proven true, so she must come to terms with the fact Max was fated to face the vampire in the tower. But did that mean Max was in the tower at this very moment?

Her grandmother's voice echoed in her head. *Time to destroy evil.*

Evil permeated this house. She'd been drawn here, and even though she didn't know how it was possible for her to destroy the vampire, she dared not delay. The time had come to try.

Before she could change her mind, she began to climb the stairs to the second floor, attempting to ignore the last vagrant wisp of doubt: what if her only purpose here was to lure Max to the mansion?

Lucy shook her head. Max was inside the house, and he needed her.

Reaching the top, she marched resolutely along the corridor to the door closing off the tower stairs. Her dimming flashlight lasted long enough to show her the door was open and then blinked out. No matter how she shook it and fiddled with the switch, the light refused to come back on.

Her heart thudding in her chest, she looked up the stairs, lighted by a faint red glow, and realized she'd seen that same sinister glow in her vision. Her lips formed Max's name, but no sound emerged.

I can't, she thought. I can't climb those steps.

Yet she knew she must. Mustering all her courage, Lucy forced herself to put her foot on the first step, as reluctant to climb to the tower room as she had been when the vampire had summoned her there. Though this time there was no outside compulsion, she was driven by an inner one, a sense arising from the bond between her and Max that told her he was in danger.

The second step. The third. When she reached the sixth step, she paused, remembering. She'd climbed no higher than the seventh step that other time. Slowly, reluctantly, she lifted her foot and placed it on the seventh step, then lifted the other to climb to the eighth. To her shock, instead of going higher, she began to sink, every bit as though the the seventh and eighth steps were not wood but quicksand. Her surroundings shifted from the tower stairs to a slimy green tunnel, where she stood up to her ankles in foul muck.

After a moment of terrified confusion, Lucy understood she'd blundered into one of the vampire's traps. With nothing familiar anywhere in sight, how could she ever find a way out?

Max struggled in vain to pry the vampire's fingers from his neck. Unable to breathe, he felt his consciousness beginning to fade. In a last desperate attempt, he shook his right arm until the gold chain slid down into his hand. With darkness threatening to overtake him, he visualized Olivia's initial as a super-heated branding iron as he pressed the *O* on the chain against the vampire's hand.

With a scream of rage and pain, the vampire released his grip, springing to his feet and holding his left hand in his right, his face twisted in agony. Max staggered to his feet, gulping air, and as his vision cleared, he saw a circle of charred flesh on the back of the vampire's hand. The stench of burned flesh filled the air.

Before Max could move, the vampire grabbed for the chain Max still held, ripping it from him and flinging the chain with its melted *O* toward the stairs.

"Your dead sister can't save you, Ryder," he said. "No one can."

Max watched him warily, edging away when the vampire took a step toward him, aware he needed time to recover from the near-fatal throttling. Even then it would be touch and go. He'd by no means regained his full strength after he'd transferred energy to save Mina and the vampire was proving to be far more powerful than he'd anticipated.

In this fight to the death, who would win?

The tunnel was lighted by a circle of white and blue lights that emitted a chill evil along their rays. Lucy, now sunk up to her knees in hideous green slime, shuddered in horror as what she'd thought were ropes hanging from the roof of the tunnel began to twist and coil in the air. Snakes! One dropped into the slime with a sickening plop and disappeared. Was it slithering toward her, hidden by the muck? In this horrible place the snake was certain to be poisonous.

Frantic, she tried to escape, but her legs were gripped fast, preventing any movement. She would, she knew in terrified resignation, die in this miasma of evil. When a grotesquely malformed golden circle suddenly appeared near the white and blue lights, she expected new horrors to plague her.

A heavy chain of gold dripped from the distorted circle to dangle in front of her. She tried to shrink away, but, as before, she couldn't move.

Climb, a woman's voice whispered, a voice she didn't recognize.

Lucy didn't trust the voice or the chain and did nothing more than eye it apprehensively. To her left, far too close, a snake's head appeared, its red eyes fixed on her as it hissed, forked tongue flicking.

Climb, the voice repeated.

With no choice left, Lucy grasped the chain, clinging to it with both hands as she struggled to free herself from the slime. The chain began to lift, pulling her up with it. Moments later, her feet were free of the foul muck. But as she neared the deadly glittering rays of the white and blue lights her head began to spin and her grip on the chain loosened.

Reject the gift, the woman's voice said.

Dizzy, afraid she was about to fall back into the slime, Lucy tried to understand what the woman meant. *Gift.* What gift? She stared at the menacing white and blue lights, bright as gems, and it came to her. Diamonds and sapphires—the bridal necklace she had worn only when he'd overcome her will and forced her to.

"I refuse the necklace you offer!" Lucy cried. "I never wanted the gift. I reject it, Vampire!"

The lights, the gold chain, the tunnel all disappeared and Lucy found herself once again standing on the stairs to the tower room. Below was darkness, above a dim red glow. As she hesitated, bewildered, she felt Max's presence near her. In the tower? He must be. With the vampire.

Taking a deep, shuddering breath, she resumed her climb. She had no idea who or what had helped her escape from the tunnel trap. Once she and Max were away from this dreadful mansion she'd ask him if he knew. She was determined, despite the vision she'd had of the tower, to keep her mind fixed on the certainty they *would* escape.

She reached the top of the stairs and stopped, gazing at a room exactly the same as the one she'd seen in her vision—the long windows, the red glow, the brass bed. And a storm raging outside. Passing quickly over this unpleasantly familiar scene, she focused on the two men circling each other near the windows.

Without thinking, she cried, "Max!"

He twisted around and stared at her. As he did, the vampire jumped him. Max stumbled backward, slamming against the window. Glass shattered. Lucy's hand flew to her mouth, stifling her gasp of horrified understanding. Her arrival had distracted Max, providing the trigger that had turned the tables against him.

Outlined by lightning's eerie glow, Max flung himself to the side, away from the broken window. Fast and powerful as a ravening wolf, the vampire leaped after him and the two men grappled, swaying back and forth as they fought for mastery.

She edged closer, skirting the brass bed, knowing with a sick revulsion that this bed was where the vampire had planned to rape and kill her once he'd summoned her to the tower. Max had saved her from that hideous fate. Somehow she must save him from the death she'd foreseen in her vision.

How? She had no way to counter the vampire's formidable power. Max, she could see, was tiring, losing ground as he tried to fend off the vampire. With a terrible, unwanted clarity, she anticipated each man's moves because she'd seen this unequal struggle before.

Appalled, she watched the vampire grasp Max by the arms and raise him from the floor. How could any man have such inhuman strength?

Inhuman, yes. The vampire was a monster.

Knuckles pressed against her mouth, she saw the vampire turn toward the open window, his intention to fling Max through it obvious. She couldn't bear to watch Max fall to his death.

"No!" she screamed, rushing toward the two men, even though she knew she couldn't reach them in time to stop the vampire.

In midflight, she felt the moonstone necklace begin to slide from her neck. Vaguely aware the clasp had given way, she automatically caught the necklace in her hand before it fell to the floor. Without conscious intention, she flung the moonstones at the vampire, now poised at the window, ready to heave Max out.

The heavy gold chain and the gems it held wrapped tightly around the vampire's neck. He staggered back, choking, dropping Max as he struggled to tear off the necklace.

Lucy fell to the floor beside Max, who sprawled on his back, urging him to move away from the window, but to her distress, she couldn't rouse him enough to make him understand. Lightning illuminated the room and she stared apprehensively at the vampire, expecting a renewed attack.

Instead she saw him stumbling drunkenly about, still trying to yank the moonstones from his throat. He wove toward them and she attempted in vain to pull Max from his path. The vampire tripped over Max's supine body and plunged forward. As thunder roared, he slammed against the broken window and fell through the empty space.

The red glow vanished, leaving the room in total darkness. Unable to believe the vampire was really gone, Lucy crept closer to the window on her hands and knees. Rain drenched her when she tried to peer out and down. She could see nothing. Surely the fall would kill him. If he could be killed. Uncertain, still apprehensive, she backed away, feeling something under one knee. Reaching down, she picked up what felt like the moonstone necklace.

Sitting back on her heels, she ran the moonstones through her fingers to make certain what she held. Max groaned. She got to her feet and was groping her way back to his side, when the next lightning flashed. Max, she saw, was attempting to sit up.

"Lucy!" Max exclaimed, reaching for her as she dropped onto her knees beside him. For a long moment they held each other close.

"Where is he?" Max asked at last. "I don't sense him anywhere."

Only then did she begin to believe the vampire might be dead. "My vision did come true," she said, "but I was wrong about the vampire winning."

CHAPTER FOURTEEN

In the tower room of the Franklin mansion, Max rose to his feet, waited until the dizziness eased and then walked unsteadily to the broken window. Windblown rain pelted him as he stared into the darkness below, unable to believe he and Lucy had triumphed over the vampire, even though he could no longer detect his presence. Gathering what energy he could muster, he started to extend his special sense in a search for any trace of the monster.

"Max," Lucy said.

Distracted, he turned toward the sound of her voice.

"I found this on the stairs," she said. A lightning flash showed her holding up a gold chain with a distorted *O* fused to it.

"My sister's," he said, taking the chain from her. "The *O* is for Olivia."

"Olivia. Your twin. So that's who she was. Olivia saved me, Max—your sister saved me. I don't understand how, but she helped me escape from the vampire's trap with that very chain. Though it seemed larger and longer at the time."

Max reached for Lucy's hand in the darkness, gripping it. "Let's get the hell out of here. We'll talk later—you can tell me about Olivia then."

As they groped their way toward the tower steps, he tried to convince himself the vampire was dead. He had to be dead. No human could have survived a fall from the tower, and no matter how powerful the vampire had become, he was still human. But a niggling doubt remained.

When they reached the steps, Max's foot crunched down on something slippery that slid from under his shoe to clatter from one step to another.

"What was that?" Lucy cried, grasping his arm.

"Your bridal necklace." Max's tone was grimmer than he'd intended.

"No! Not mine! Your sister told me to reject it and I did. Otherwise I couldn't have escaped from the trap."

Relief coursed through him. The diamond-and-sapphire necklace no longer was a threat. Although even if Lucy hadn't rejected it, with the vampire dead the necklace wasn't dangerous. Still, as they descended the steps, no matter how hard he tried to convince himself they were safe, his unease persisted.

"The trap I fell into was between the seventh and eighth steps from the bottom," Lucy warned.

"Don't worry about it," Max advised. "Because you escaped, the trap's defused."

By the time they came to the bottom of the tower steps, the lightning flashed less often and he realized the storm must be moving north. Darkness complicated their passage along the upstairs corridor toward the back staircase, increasing Max's premonition of danger.

They finally arrived at the rear door, but when he opened it the chain he'd draped over his left arm suddenly grew very warm, triggering his special sense. He halted in the kitchen with Lucy beside him while he scanned the area immediately outside.

"What's wrong?" she asked.

Leaning close, he spoke into her ear. "Don't talk."

He felt her tension mount, until it matched his own. Time stood still for him as he stretched his probe farther and farther.

There! He sensed an aberrant, no doubt about it. The vampire? The signal was too faint for him to be sure. The bastard must be dead; he could be picking up someone else, someone who had minimal ability.

He'd known all along he'd never be satisfied until he actually found the vampire's body and proved to himself beyond a shadow of a doubt that the monster was truly dead. Would the body lie where it should be, on the ground under the broken window of the tower? Dread settled over him like a shroud.

He tugged at Lucy's hand, urging her to follow him through the doorway and into the night. The storm had passed on. Mist rather than rain dampened his face and the moon shone dimly through the thinning clouds as he and Lucy began to circle the house at enough distance away so he could locate the broken window. Her grip on his hand tightened, but she remained silent while they went round.

The moon broke through, casting silver light on the tower, clearly showing the broken window. A thorough search underneath revealed no sign of the vampire or his body.

"Damn!" Max muttered. That he'd been expecting this made it no easier to accept.

As he tried to decide what to do next, Lucy whispered urgently, "Look at Olivia's chain."

He glanced down in time to see the now-shining chain snap free of his arm. To his amazement, instead of falling it floated several feet above the ground, slowly drifting away from them. Lucy recovered quicker than he did, pulling him with her as she followed the shining broken chain toward the shed where Max had taken shelter earlier.

Lucy hesitated when they neared the shed. "I feel him," she whispered. "How can he still be alive?"

No mere mortal can kill me. The words blazed into Max's mind. Lucy's gasp said she'd also received the vampire's unspoken message.

Max's extra sense told him the bastard was inside the shed. The signal was weaker than usual, though, so weak that Max suspected the fall must have injured him. Had the fall also diminished his powers? Max hoped so. The vampire, weakened, would still be formidable. Max faced a dilemma. If he and Lucy didn't remain physically linked, he worried that the vampire might overpower her. On the other hand, if he didn't release her hand, he'd have to face the vampire encumbered.

His sister's chain, hovering near the closed door of the shed, shone against the weathered wood as though seeking entrance. Why? Did his images of her within the links still seek revenge? Even if that were true, he feared Olivia's chain would prove no more than a minor distraction to the vampire.

No matter how exhausted he was, Max couldn't turn away, leaving the vampire alive. They had to have a confrontation here and now. Since he sensed a trap connected with the door, he didn't dare pull it open, and he'd lost too much energy to attempt to defuse the trap. The vampire must be lured into the open.

"You're human, Vampire," he called. "No human is immortal. You may have survived the fall, but I challenge you to survive combat with me!"

Lucy drew in her breath sharply. In reaction to his words? Max glanced at her. She'd reclasped the moonstone necklace around her neck and the gems glowed with power. When he faced the vampire, he hoped he could tap into that power—God knows he needed it. And more.

Silence fell. Not a sound disturbed the night.

Lucy leaned to him and whispered in his ear. "I love you, Max." Her words penetrated to his heart, where he cherished them, even though he realized why she'd spoken. She feared neither of them would survive the vampire's attack. She might well be right.

Though he'd resolved never to tell her how he felt, chilled by the danger they faced, he understood if he didn't speak now, he and she could both die without her knowing. He risked gathering her close for one sweet moment, murmuring to her, "I'll never love anyone but you."

As he released her, the shed door slammed open. Moonlight illuminated the vampire's malevolent smile.

"You die first, Ryder." The words coiled in the air, poisonous as snakes. "And you'll die knowing Lucy's mine."

Mesmerized into immobility by the vampire's terrifying prediction, Lucy watched as the shining chain drifted from the shed door to form a golden halo above his head. Intent on Max, he gave no sign he noticed.

He looks like the caricature of an angel, Lucy thought. A fallen angel, a devil who meant first to kill Max and then to torture and despoil her before he killed her. Aware through their bond of Max's weakened energy, she despaired.

If she called on Medea for help, the kitten might die. Who else was there? Remembering how she'd escaped from the slime trap, she recognized a possibility. With no assurance she could reach her, she fixed her gaze on the chain and begged, *Help Max, Olivia. Help the brother you loved.*

The vampire pointed his index finger at Max. Though nothing visible showed, to Lucy's horror Max stumbled backward, losing his grip on her hand. The vampire limped forward—how badly was he hurt? she wondered. Evidently not enough to stop him. The halo remained with him as the vampire intoned words Lucy didn't understand, words that forced Max to his knees.

Lucy felt Max's effort as he struggled to his feet and faced the vampire, and wished she knew how to lend him energy.

"You'll have to do better than that," Max told the vampire. As he spoke, he brought his right knee up abruptly, ramming it into the vampire's groin.

The vampire doubled over, grunting in pain, and Max brought his clasped hands down hard on the back of the vampire's neck, felling him, facedown. Max dropped on top of him, hooking an arm around his throat and pulling back. The vampire choked and gagged. But then, in a movement so swift he seemed to Lucy to blur, the vampire flipped over onto his back, breaking the choke hold and pinning Max beneath him.

A knife materialized in the vampire's hand, from where Lucy had no idea. He sprang to his feet and, knife in hand, lunged at Max, who'd gotten onto one knee. Max flung himself to one side, missing the thrust meant for his heart. The knife grazed his arm, drawing blood.

The vampire howled in triumph. Why, Lucy didn't understand, since Max was barely wounded. One glance at Max's stricken face, though, warned her that the shallow knife cut had put him at risk. Did it have something to do with blood?

The vampire edged away, tipped his head back and raised the bloody blade of the knife to his mouth to catch a drop of Max's blood. As he did, Olivia's chain whipped down, deflecting the drop of blood, then slid into the vampire's open mouth and vanished from Lucy's sight.

The vampire dropped the knife, his scream strangling in his throat as he clawed futilely at his neck.

As you did, so I do, a woman's voice said.

The vampire staggered in circles, moaning in agony, finally falling to his knees, obviously in terrible pain. At last he sprawled onto his side, where he lay unmoving. Lucy, staring in amazement at the smoke rising from his clothes, started when Max put his arm around her. Seeing the vampire burst into flames, she covered her mouth with her hand, aghast.

"He burned Olivia," Max explained, the sadness and anger in his voice tinged with a certain satisfaction at the justice Olivia had reached from beyond the grave to mete out. "He claimed no mortal alive could kill him—but he forgot the dead."

Though aware Max would need to watch to the very end to make certain the vampire was destroyed, Lucy couldn't bear the sight and turned away. Max drew her into his arms and she pressed her face against his chest until it was over.

Not until they were in her car with Max driving over the storm-wracked roads did she remember confessing that she loved him. She recalled very clearly what he'd said to her in return, that he'd never love anyone else. She hugged his words to her, taking comfort from them as she struggled to banish the night's horrors.

Eventually Mina's abduction came to her mind. "What happened to Mina?" she asked, afraid of what Max might tell her.

"I'm almost sure she'll be okay," he said, without adding any details.

Reassured, Lucy fell silent.

Once they reached the cottage, Max came in with her. Glancing into the box at the cats, he said, "I see Persy and Medea are doing well."

"I didn't call on them for help," she said. "I asked your sister, instead." She bit her lip as the memory of the flames flared into her mind.

"He deserved what he got," Max said grimly. "Don't think about it anymore. You're exhausted— time to get some rest."

Since they'd already been sharing her bed in one way or another, Lucy expected Max would continue to do so. But he didn't—at least not as she'd imagined he would. He waited for her to crawl under the covers and then sat beside her, fully dressed, holding her hand. She wanted to ask why, but overcome by fatigue, she couldn't prevent her eyelids from drooping shut and then sleep crept up and claimed her.

Lucy awoke to the grayness of early morning. Alone. Feeling abandoned, she assured herself that she'd find Max in the kitchen, but the only thing she discovered there was a note telling her he'd taken her car because he had to meet Ford.

If he had her car, he'd have to return, she thought, then wondered why she'd put it that way. He'd return even if he didn't have her car! They were bonded. For life, he'd insisted. Of course he'd come back to her.

After downing coffee and toast, she fed Persy and sat by the box, watching the kitten crawl blindly about searching for her missing mother. Stroking the tiny head with her forefinger, she spoke softly to Medea.

"We've survived the vampire. Now you have nothing to do but eat and sleep and grow into the most beautiful cat in the world."

Later, as she dressed, Lucy began to realize the truth of her words. They *had* survived the vampire, she and the cats and Max. The monster who'd called himself "Joe Dooley" had been totally destroyed—he'd never return.

She was free!

Crossing to the dresser, she ran her fingers over the moonstone necklace, her heritage from her grandmother, a bequest that had helped to save them all. If she put it around her neck would she have a vision of the future? Of her and Max together? Though she was tempted, Lucy turned away. Somehow she was afraid to look ahead.

The morning passed slowly. Shortly before noon Polly came over to check on Persy.

"I've made up my mind to have her spayed as soon as she's through nursing that kitten," Polly said. "She's borne enough litters."

So Medea *was* Persy's last kitten, exactly as Max had said, Lucy thought. "I do hope you'll let me have the kitten," she said to Polly.

"I'm happy to have you take it off my hands." Polly peered into the box. "My, it's a tiny one."

"She's getting stronger every day," Lucy insisted.

"A female, is it? Frankly I prefer females, even if one kitten after another does get to be a nuisance. Toms are a tad too macho for my taste. Which reminds me." She paused and glanced around the kitchen. "I know it's none of my business, but then again, in a way, since he's been staying at my place, it is."

When Polly didn't go on, Lucy said, "Are you talking about Max?"

"Then he *has* moved in with you."

Taken aback, Lucy echoed her words. "Moved in?"

"I realize he's been spending nights here to make sure you weren't disturbed by that shifty-eyed Joe Dooley." Polly threw her an arch look that said as clearly as words that she suspected there was more to those nights than Max's guarding Lucy. "But when he took all his belongings out of my house early this morning," Polly went on, "I couldn't help but wonder if he planned to move in with you permanently."

Beyond speech, Lucy shook her head.

"Oh, dear!" Polly exclaimed. "I can tell by your expression that he isn't here. I've gone and put my foot

in it, haven't I? Was it because your brother objected?''

Lucy pulled herself together. "Ford isn't involved.
And, for that matter, neither are Max and I." Despite
her effort to speak calmly, her voice shook.

Polly reached over and patted her hand. "Never you
mind, dear. I always say whatever happens is for the
best in the long run.''

After Polly left, Lucy sat at the kitchen table staring dispiritedly into the dregs of her coffee. *For the
best.* Is that what Max had believed when he'd removed all his things from Polly's and left without a
word?

Hearing a car pull up alongside her house, she
jumped to her feet. When she looked and saw Ford
uncoil himself from behind the wheel of her small car,
disappointment turned down the corners of her
mouth.

"I don't have time for coffee," her brother said as
he entered the cottage. "Pete's coming by to pick me
up.''

Pete, she knew, was one of his deputies.

"Thought you might need your car," Ford added,
tossing the keys on the hall stand. "Hell of a mess all
around last night. We're still trying to sort things out.
We did find Mina, you know.''

Ashamed because she hadn't given Mina another
thought until this moment, Lucy said, "How is she?''

"Recovering. I never did believe Ryder had anything to do with her abduction, but I was glad when
she woke up enough to clear him. I'd hate to force him
to stay here any longer than necessary.''

Did that mean Max had already left? Lucy couldn't bring herself to ask.

Ford pulled her into his arms and hugged her. "I have him to thank for saving my little sister from Dooley," he said gruffly as he released her. "You're okay, aren't you, Sis? You know it's all over as far as you're concerned."

All over. The words rang in her ears as she summoned a far-from-genuine smile. "I'm fine."

A horn honked outside. "That's Pete," Ford said. "See you later." He hurried from the house.

Feeling more alone than she ever had in her life, Lucy tried to make herself keep busy, but failed dismally. The day dragged into evening, a warm and pleasant evening that might just as well have been wet and miserable as far as she was concerned. She stood in the open back door, looking at the rising moon. When Persy wandered over and sat expectantly at her feet, obviously waiting to be let out, Lucy pushed open the screen and exited with the cat.

"Beware of owls," she warned Persy as the cat trotted toward the magnolia tree.

Why didn't anyone advise me to beware of love? Lucy asked herself as she trailed after the cat.

She sighed. Undoubtedly she wouldn't have paid attention any more than Persy did to her warning about owls. Even if she had, what good would it have done? Love couldn't be, wouldn't be, denied. Love swept in uninvited and lodged in your heart.

How could she ever have imagined she was in love with the false Joe Dooley? Her feeling for him hadn't even come close to the overwhelming emotion Max evoked within her.

She found Persy diligently covering up the hole she'd dug near the magnolia. "Remember when I was a cat and we were up in this tree?" she asked her, belatedly recalling it had been a dream.

Is that what her time with Max had been—no more than a dream?

"He said it was impossible to break our bond," she told Persy.

"No more than the truth."

Until he appeared from behind the magnolia, Lucy couldn't be sure Max's voice wasn't speaking inside her head.

"I promised to always tell you the truth," he added. "I keep my promises."

He stood no more than two feet from her, moonlight silvering his face without revealing his expression.

"Damn it, Lucy," he said, "I've met my match in you. I tried to leave, but—"

When he didn't go on, she said, "I didn't stop you."

"The hell you didn't. I can no more leave you than I can leave myself behind. You're a part of me." He took a step toward her. "When I told you that I could never love anyone else, I half expected to die at the hands of the vampire. Instead, he's dead, I'm still here and I still feel exactly the same. You said then that you loved me—was it the truth?"

He'd told her the truth, she would do the same. "Yes," she whispered.

Closing the gap between them, he wrapped his arms around her. As his lips met hers, the bond between them activated and Lucy felt the warmth of his love surround her, and knew that he was equally aware of her love for him.

Plaintive wails interrupted their kiss, Persy letting them know that she felt returning to her kitten was far more urgent than their lovemaking.

"I swore I'd never marry," Max said as he walked toward the cottage with his arm around Lucy.

"I don't recall asking you," she said tartly.

He stopped abruptly, turning her to face him. "Damn it, *I'm* asking *you!*"

"Even though you swore you never would?" she teased.

"I don't have a choice—as you very well know."

"Ah, but *I* do."

Max pulled her against him. "So you think you have a choice," he said huskily. "I have news for you. We were both doomed from the moment we met— appropriately enough at the altar." His mouth slanted over hers in a kiss that, shared through their bond, sent her sailing into another world, until Persy's strong objection to the delay brought her back to reality.

"June, I think," Lucy murmured against Max's lips before he reluctantly let her go.

"I guarantee no interruptions at our wedding," he said as they walked hand in hand to the cottage. "I plan to lock all the church doors to make sure."

CHAPTER FIFTEEN

"I'm so glad you decided to have the wedding at St. John's," Katie said to Lucy as they sat over coffee in Lucy's kitchen. "I was afraid you might not want to because of—well, you know."

"I wanted a church wedding," Lucy said, "because this time I'm truly in love with the man I'm marrying. This time the marriage is for real." She smiled at Katie. "And you can be sure you and the other bridesmaids won't have to wear blue again!"

"You're so radiant. It's plain to see Max really is your true love. And from the way he looks at you I can tell he's as besotted as you are." Katie sighed.

Katie's sad expression brought Lucy out of her cloud of happiness. She leaned forward. "What's the matter?"

Katie sighed again. "Luke asked me to marry him."

Lucy gazed at her in surprise. "Why so unhappy? Why aren't you jumping for joy? Have you turned him down?"

"How can I?" Tears glistened in Katie's eyes. "You know I love Luke."

"Then what's the problem?" Even as she asked, Lucy remembered Luke's confession when she'd told him about her vision. She wondered if he'd shared with Katie what he'd admitted to her.

"You said your marriage is for real, and anyone can see it's the truth." A tear escaped to roll down Katie's cheek. "My marriage to Luke won't be for real in any sense of the word. I know he's not marrying me for love, but only because he needs a mother for his son. Up until now I've always been a bridesmaid. Though my time has finally come, I won't be a true bride—I'll be a mere convenience."

Lucy, her heart aching, understanding she alone knew Luke's secret, one she was honor bound not to reveal, rose and pulled Katie up so she could try to comfort her with a hug. How she wished she could lend her friend some of her own overwhelming joy....

Days later, when Lucy stood before the altar at St. John's with Max beside her, she had no room for poor Katie's unhappiness. The love she saw in Max's eyes as he gazed down at her surrounded her, filling her heart completely.

Just before he'd led her down the aisle to join Max, Ford had whispered, "He's the right man for you, Sis. I can feel it in my bones."

Lucy knew she would have married Max even if the entire world had been against them. She didn't need her brother's approval, but she was warmed to know he'd given it. Nor did she need the comfort of her grandmother's moonstone necklace, which she wore around her neck. She'd decided, though, if the faulty link held throughout the ceremony rather than giving way, it would mean she and Max had her grandmother's approval, as well.

Hands clasped, she and Max faced each other, when suddenly, for an instant so brief she could hardly believe what she'd seen, a golden *O* formed in the air between them, vanishing almost immediately.

The look in Max's eyes told Lucy he understood and was as touched as she that Olivia somehow knew of their happiness and had found a way to bless their union.

*   *   *   *   *

Turn the page for a sneak preview of

FINALLY A BRIDE
by Sherryl Woods,

the last book in the
Always a Bridesmaid! series....

CHAPTER ONE

"Marry me."

The two simple, totally unexpected words hit Katie Jones with the force of a tornado. If Luke had asked her to join him on a shuttle to the moon, she wouldn't have been more stunned. Katie was suddenly very glad they weren't in plain sight. At least there was no one around to see her mouth drop open, no one to witness in case she followed through on her urge to whap him upside his hard head with a frying pan. If Luke Cassidy had asked her to marry him six years ago, she would have wept with joy. Today that same request— that out-of-the-blue mockery of a proposal—filled her with fury.

"You want to marry me?" she replied incredulously. Her pulse, apparently unaware that the proposal merited anger, not consideration, took off as if this were a declaration of true love. "Six years without a word and now you want to marry me?"

"Just like that," he agreed as calmly as if the suggestion weren't totally absurd.

"Have you lost your mind?"

He seemed to consider the question thoughtfully, then shook his head, his expression thoroughly serious. "Nope. I don't think so."

"Then I think you need a second opinion."

"Katie, I have given this a lot of thought. It makes sense."

She regarded him blankly. "Why?" she asked, when she should have been shrieking to the high heavens about the gall of any man who would walk back into a woman's life after six years and drop a marriage proposal on the table as if it were a simple hello.

"Why?" she asked again, wondering if there was any chance she would get the simple, three-word answer she'd always dreamed of hearing cross his lips.

"My son needs a mother. You need somebody to put this place on a sound financial base again. We always got along. I think we could make it work."

Not three words, but a litany, Katie noticed in disgust as Luke ticked off the reasons matter-of-factly. He'd probably made a damn list of them. His business-like tone made her grind her teeth.

"You sound as if you're negotiating for the merger of two companies with compatible products," she accused.

The idiot didn't even have the decency to deny it.

"That's one way of looking at it, I suppose," he agreed, looking pleased that she had grasped the concept. "We both get something we need. I knew I could count on you not to get all sloppy and sentimental about this."

Katie was just itching to reach for that cast-iron skillet that was sitting atop her twenty-year-old stove when she made the mistake of looking again into Luke's eyes. Those blue eyes that had once danced with laughter were flat and empty now. Lonely. Lost.

Katie had always been a sucker for a lost soul. And from her twelfth birthday, when he'd brought her a wilted, but flamboyantly huge bouquet of wildflowers, she had been a sucker for Luke Cassidy. Regrettably nothing in the last six years they'd been apart had changed that.

She drew in a deep, steadying breath and realized that she was going to do it. She was going to say yes and damn the consequences....

Always a Bridesmaid!

MILLION DOLLAR SWEEPSTAKES (III)

No purchase necessary. To enter, follow the directions published. Method of entry may vary. For eligibility, entries must be received no later than March 31, 1996. No liability is assumed for printing errors, lost, late or misdirected entries. Odds of winning are determined by the number of eligible entries distributed and received. Prizewinners will be determined no later than June 30, 1996.

Sweepstakes open to residents of the U.S. (except Puerto Rico), Canada, Europe and Taiwan who are 18 years of age or older. All applicable laws and regulations apply. Sweepstakes offer void wherever prohibited by law. Values of all prizes are in U.S. currency. This sweepstakes is presented by Torstar Corp., its subsidiaries and affiliates, in conjunction with book, merchandise and/or product offerings. For a copy of the Official Rules send a self-addressed, stamped envelope (WA residents need not affix return postage) to: MILLION DOLLAR SWEEPSTAKES (III) Rules, P.O. Box 4573, Blair, NE 68009, USA.

EXTRA BONUS PRIZE DRAWING

No purchase necessary. The Extra Bonus Prize will be awarded in a random drawing to be conducted no later than 5/30/96 from among all entries received. To qualify, entries must be received by 3/31/96 and comply with published directions. Drawing open to residents of the U.S. (except Puerto Rico), Canada, Europe and Taiwan who are 18 years of age or older. All applicable laws and regulations apply; offer void wherever prohibited by law. Odds of winning are dependent upon number of eligibile entries received. Prize is valued in U.S. currency. The offer is presented by Torstar Corp., its subsidiaries and affiliates in conjunction with book, merchandise and/or product offering. For a copy of the Official Rules governing this sweepstakes, send a self-addressed, stamped envelope (WA residents need not affix return postage) to: Extra Bonus Prize Drawing Rules, P.O. Box 4590, Blair, NE 68009, USA.

SWP-S895

Become a Privileged Woman,
You'll be entitled to all these Free Benefits. And Free Gifts, too.

To thank you for buying our books, we've designed an exclusive FREE program called *PAGES & PRIVILEGES™*. You can enroll with just one Proof of Purchase, and get the kind of luxuries that, until now, you could only read about.

BIG HOTEL DISCOUNTS

A privileged woman stays in the finest hotels. And so can you—at up to 60% off! Imagine standing in a hotel check-in line and watching as the guest in front of you pays $150 for the same room that's only costing you $60. Your *Pages & Privileges* discounts are good at Sheraton, Marriott, Best Western, Hyatt and thousands of other fine hotels all over the U.S., Canada and Europe.

FREE DISCOUNT TRAVEL SERVICE

A privileged woman is always jetting to romantic places.

When you fly, just make one phone call for the lowest published airfare at time of booking— or double the difference back!

PLUS—you'll get a $25 voucher to use the first time you book a flight AND 5% cash back on every ticket you buy thereafter through the travel service!

PROOF OF PURCHASE
Offer expires October 31, 1996

SS-PP51